NICHOLAS II

Story of an Oaktown O. G.

A Storm is Coming

A B HUDSON

A B Hudson

BOSS UP PUBLISHING

ISBN: 978-157276845

Acknowledgments

First and foremost, I give thanks to God and my Savior Jesus Christ, for giving me the wisdom and clarity to pen this story. I honor my wife for patiently bearing all the long nights of constant skirmishes. Her gracious help in researching and examining facts and subject matter. Her help in recognizing and simplifying characters was insurmountable. Her comments and feedback provided background into the substance to the characters. My special thanks and appreciation to my daughter, for her discernment as to how her generation may review and except my opinions, I say, thank you. To my loyal friends and fans that enjoyed my writing, thank you for your patience; to those of you who are experiencing my writing for the first time, please enjoy and I hope you will become a loyal fan in the future. To the many fans who enjoyed my first book you have patiently waited, I cannot thank you enough for your patience, reviews, and comments. I hope that everyone enjoys this writing as much as I enjoyed writing it.

Thank you very much.

Table of Content

Prologue

Saturday morning in the parking lot of the Alameda Golf Course, sat a stolen brown Plymouth, four door Fury, with three men, waiting for Nicholas to finish his round of golf; William Franklin a white want to be pimp, with two Mexicans named Oscar and his partner Juan, both from Houston. They sat in the Plymouth and waited, as the information they had gotten was good.

The information was that Nicholas would finish about ten. They planned to hit him and get the hell out of dodge before anyone knew what happened. They had tried to hit him Friday night at the Showcase night club. But as luck would have it, just as they were going to pull up and open fire, a cop car pulled up beside them at the light. So, they had to back off. But today they were going to get the job done.

Nicholas and three men were walking from the club house to the parking lot. One of them was talking to Nicholas as they carried their clubs to the car.

"I have you shooting a 70 with two birdies and a sand save Nick... Dick you shot 74...Jerry you shot 78...and I shot 79, so we owe Nick three-hundred and fifty each", said Ted, with a little attitude in his voice, as he put his clubs in the trunk of his BMW. Nick continued walking to his car which was next to Ted's, but four lanes over from the Plymouth in the lot.

"I thought Nicholas drove that Black El Dorado, pointing at the black Eldorado one lane over from the Plymouth", said William, mad because he was parked too far away.

"Damn it, start up so we can catch him on the way out," said Oscar, from the passenger seat, as he watched Nick put his clubs in the trunk of his chocolate brown and tan Eldorado. The other men were doing the same, putting their clubs in their cars, preparing to leave. "I'll will see you later today Ted...Good round today, let's play Hayward on Wednesday," stated Nick, from the trunk of his car, with a smile.

"That'll be cool, maybe I can win back some of my bread", said Ted, with a disgusting look on his face, standing next to his beamer.

"I have a 7:10 am tee time... is that okay with you?", replied Nick.

"Yeah, that's fine, I will call Dick and Jerry... Now I have to go check on my ladies and get my money", replied Ted, as he got in his car to leave.

Nick got in his caddy and started to drive off. He had to get home and change. He also wanted to get Nina some roses from the flower shop downtown.

Unlike other days, he was not on his game. His mind was on Nina coming home. He didn't see the Plymouth trying to catch up to him, as he continued to drive down Otis road towards the High Street drawbridge. He made it onto the bridge, just as the barrage gate started down. The signal light changed to red behind him. He made it safely across and continued on his way home.

***

By the time William was about to catch up to the caddy, Nick had a four-car lead on him. William was trying to catch him but with the traffic and how Nicholas was driving, William was unable to gain any ground on the caddy, as it headed down Otis Road towards the High Street drawbridge.

"Get closer to him... don't lose him... we have to get this son of a bitch and get the hell out of town," said Oscar, in an excited voice.

"I'm trying to get closer, don't you see all these cars in front of me...what you want me to do run over them?" , said William, as he tried to close the space between the van and the caddy.

Then as they turned onto the approach to the drawbridge, the signal started flashing and the barricade came down. The bridge started to rise to allow a couple of sail boats to pass under it. The three cars in front of William started to break for the barricade as the bridge started to raise. Nicholas made it over the bridge before the signal started and the barricade dropped.

They once again lost an opportunity, because by the time the barricade was raised, Nicholas car had disappeared. William continued on up High Street to the freeway and headed back to the city. Oscar was mad as hell and thought to himself, he should have just got out in the lot and shot Nicholas in the head right there in the lot.

***

Chapter 1

Oscar yelled, "That's them right there!" Oscar said, from the passenger seat.

"Wait! Let me pull up next to them, then tap that ass," replied William, trying his best to sound tough.

Oscar climbed into the back, while Juan picked up a 9-mm Israel UZI off the seat and flipped the safety off, while getting in position to shoot out the van side door.

"Get us close and then get the hell out of here, understand," Oscar said, to William, as if he knew what he was doing. He picked up the other UZI and flipped off the safety and got set to fire out the door.

Oscar pulled the door handle and slid the van door open as William moved the van into the lane next to the caddy. They both slid the level back, loading the first round into their UZI's. They were so nervous that they both were sweating as if they just got out of a shower. "Wait, let me get closer before you open that door," said William, as he could barely see Nicholas driving through the dark tinted windows. As he got to the front window of the caddy, he yelled, "Now do it, light him up."

Within the bat-of-an-eye the two men in the rear of the van opened fire, pointed their UZI's out the van's side door, aiming at the Cadillac driver, and pulled the trigger.

Rat-tat! Rat-tat! Rat-tat! Rat-tat! Rat-tat! Rat-tat! Rat-tat! Rat-tat! Rat-tat! Rat-tat! Rat-tat! Rat-tat!

The driver of the Cadillac made a hard right as bullets started to rip holes into the side of the caddy.

***

The loud sound of the Uzi's firing and bullet casings flying made William panic and step on the gas, causing the van to burn rubber. Barely able to control the van and hold it on the road, William's attention turned to getting away. The two gunmen closed the side door and sat back in the seat.

"We hit him, did you see the way he jumped when that hot shit hit him?" said Oscar, looking out the back window of the van, to see if anyone was following them.

"Yes, I hit him at least a dozen times," replied Juan, as the van headed towards the airport exit. William looked in the driver side mirror, and then the passenger mirror to see if anyone was following. Seeing nothing, he changed lanes and headed to the south entrance to the freeway headed south.

***

William headed towards San Jose, staying under the speed limit. His heart, however, would not slow down, heaving in his chest, as if it were going to break out, his mind was racing a mile a minute; he just couldn't get a handle on his emotions and paranoia was taking hold. His knuckles had turned white from squeezing the steering wheel tightly, he was not aware he was sweating like he had just run a marathon.

It was obvious he was scared and apprehensive about the shooting, *"What am I doing here. I'm not a killer. I have never shot anybody in my life. Now here I am driving this damn van."* He was having a hell of a time with his mind. He hadn't shot or been in the vicinity of a shooting in his life.

Yeah, he thought he was a bad boy, but the truth remained, he was just a little rich boy playing bad. He was a ho's trick daddy and a street clown. He wanted to be a pimp and act like the people he saw in the movies. However, real life is not like the movies and he was getting a real-life lesson first hand. Now he was involved in a killing and wanted for murder.

He thought as he drove. *"What if we get caught, would Oscar and Juan say he did the shooting? I didn't shoot anyone or handled the gun. I just drove this van. Wait, what if they decide to shoot me to keep me from talking?"* All kinds of things were running through his mind as he drove.

Nicholas II A Storm is Coming

Paranoia setting in rapidly, his mind was thinking of movies he had seen. Movies where the killers crossed their partner's, killing everyone who knew anything. He didn't know if Oscar or Juan had orders to get rid of him after he set up Nicholas.

***

Getting off the freeway on University and Bay shore Avenue in East Palo Alto, William drove down a dimly lighted street. Finding a vacant lot next to a building, he pulled the van in and cut the engine off. The three of them got out and took two five-gallon cans of gas and started to drench the van inside and out with the gas. After they were satisfied, they had soaked the van, they threw the gas cans back in the van. Walking a safe distance from the van. Oscar took a book of matches and lit it, then threw it at the van.

The fumes from the gas ignited in a flash, sending flames reaching to the night sky. They walked away as the frames ingulfed the van and lit up the street. Making their way unseen to the corner, they headed to the gas station, as the first sirens could be heard from the fire trucks and police.

***

J uan walked into the store, walked up to the counter, and asked the clerk for a pack of Newport's. Oscar stuck his head in the door and said, "Hey Juan, get me a bag of chips and something to drink."

William walked to the phone booth and called Susan, his main woman. He gave her some directions over the phone and hung up. William wanted to get the fuck away from Oscar and Juan as fast as he could but had to wait for Susan to pick him up. He thought about how long it would take her to drive from the city; along with the fact that the police were driving around looking for anything or anyone looking suspicious.

He spotted the little bar across the street from the gas station. William suggested they needed to wait for Susan in the bar and get off the street. Susan told him she would be there within ninety minutes.

Still paranoid and scared, he waited nervously for Susan. Given all the shit running through his mind, he was a cold mess. He knew it was to his best interest to get the fuck out of town, as soon as possible.

Juan walked out the store to find Oscar and William sitting on a broke down bench next to the phone booth. Oscar took the chips, opening them, popping one in his mouth, and said, "we should go over to that bar and wait on your bitch," to William, with a little attitude.

Juan looked across the street at the bar and thought it was a bad idea. They had no idea who or what kind of people were in that joint. But it was going to take time for Susan to drive from the city. Besides, they were not going anywhere until they got the rest of their money. They didn't need to be out in the streets with the police driving around and fire trucks around the corner. They decided it was wise to walk over to the bar and have a beer while they waited for Susan.

***

They had been in the bar about an hour when William spotted Susan walking in the front door. William got up from the table and met her in front of the bar, they walked back to the table and sat down. "Hey baby, did you bring that package I told you to get?", asked William, loud enough for Susan to hear over the jukebox.

"Yes, I have it out back in the car. Want me to bring it in here?", she replied, with a questioning look in her eyes as she looked around the bar. There was only a hand full of people in the bar and none of them were paying them any attention. They were watching some fight on the big TV screen.

"No, we are going to go out and get in the car, just let me finish this beer", said William, as he turned up the bottle.

"Does she have our money you promised?", asked Juan, with excitement in his voice.

"Yes, finish your beer and let's go out to the car. I will give you your share and we can get out of here", stated William, trying to sound like he was a boss.

Oscar and Juan got in the back seat while William got behind the wheel. Susan reached for the briefcase on the passenger seat and sat it on her lap.

William opened the case on her lap and took out two cellophane wrapped bundles; each bundle was forty-thousand dollars. William handed one bundle to Oscar and one to Juan.

"There you go fellows, your share, now it has been all good, but I have to go. It's almost nine, so, if I were you, I would get to San Jose, and catch a flight back to Houston," said William, hoping they would get out of his car so he could get in the wind himself.

Getting out the car Oscar thought to himself "I should put one in his ear and fuck that bitch," but decided he had better get back to Houston as he was told. So, he opened the door and got out followed by Juan.

Oscar walked over to the gas station's phone and called a cab. He wanted to get out of the area and back to Houston. While on the phone he turned to Juan and said, "the cab will be here in about ten minutes."

"We need to go back to the motel and get our stuff and then get to the airport and leave", replied Juan, with a hint of nerves and fear in his voice.

"Yeah, but we can't go to the same airport we just did a hit at," questioned Juan still tripping about the airport.

"Who said we were going to that airport…. We are going to go to San Jose and catch a plane out of there," said Oscar, like he knew what he was saying.

***

When the cab arrived at the gas station, Oscar and Juan told the driver to take them to their motel. They needed to get their belongings before heading to the airport. At the motel, they told the driver to wait, went in, and got their stuff; climbed back in the cab and told the driver to take them to the San Jose airport. Sitting in the cab Oscar started to think about making a move to Cali and setting up shop. He thought about setting up his own trap house and being his own boss. The more he thought about it, the more he liked the idea.

Mainly because from what he had seen of the local dope boys and their game, they were weak and didn't have a strong game. Given the two main guys he had dealt with, P-Slim and his partner Dirty Mike, two wannabes from Oaktown who helped set up Nicholas.

Juan was also sitting back, thinking about buying a new Chrysler New Yorker and getting him some ho's. Thinking about being a bad-ass pimp with money, he could now buy the clothes. With a bad car and money, he could get ho's to pay him some attention.

Flip Haynes, his mother's older brother was now going to have to give him respect. Now having hit Nicholas, he was a made man, a cold-hearted killer, he thought in his mind. Yes, a great deal ran through both of their heads while the cab headed south towards San Jose.

***

Chapter 3

S everal gunshots rained from a black van in the lane next to Nicholas. His street and survival instincts jumped into action as he veered the Cadillac to the right, away from the gun fire. Nicholas instinctively reached out to try and protect Nina, as unimaginable pain from the bullets started ripping his skin apart. The heavy slugs tore into his bones on the left side of his jaw line. Nicholas tried to yell, "Nina duck," as he veered right into the path of a car in the right lane.

The Cadillac hit the light pole with so much force the front end whipped around the base of the pole. The last thing Nicholas remembered was the light pole looking as big as a tree and then everything went black.

* * *

The man in a car behind the Cadillac, in the right lane, slammed on his brakes coming to an abrupt stop. Had it not been for quick reaction he would have slammed into the passenger side of the Cadillac, as it veered right into his lane, before ramming into the light pole.

He had seen the flash of the gun fire and heard the gun shots coming from the black van in front of him. He was shocked and afraid for his own life. He had heard about people shooting at each other in the streets, but never in a million years, did he ever think he would be witness to it.

However, his adrenaline is flowing so hard he seems to be moving under some strange force. Before he knew what was happening, he had jumped out of his car, running to the driver's side of the Cadillac. He tried to pull open the driver's door, but it would not budge. Thinking fast he ran around to the passenger side, where he was able to pull open the door getting the woman's seat belt off and holding her by her shoulders, he drug her out of the car, and over to the side of the road, as other people had begun to stop. They all assisted in trying to get the man out of the car.

A police officer on his way to work at the airport police station, coming from the opposite direction of the incident, heard the gun shots. He saw the black van and the Caddy on the opposite side of the road, hearing the shots and the sound of tires screeching on the road. He made a U-turn about three cars behind the incident scene. With his lights on he pulled up behind cars that were now stopping to see what happened.

The officer took hold of the microphone and called the dispatcher, "G-54 I have shots fired at the airport exit road", Code 2, I have shots fired at the exit road of the airport. Black van headed west on the exit road. One car hit light pole." Pulling up in a way as to block off the two lanes, he jumped out of his car and ran to the site.

He was able to see blood coming from the woman's neck. She was lying on the ground next to the road barrier and someone had placed a coat over her. She looked to be unconscious, but alive. At first glance, he saw the man was still in the car and blood was everywhere. He could not determine if he were dead or alive. From the looks of the car, the driver's side fender and door had a lot of bullet holes.

***

As other police cars arrived at the scene, the first officer, who initially called in the shooting was trying to get the man out of the driver's side of the car and telling others to pull the door open. He tried everything in his power to open the door, but it would not budge or give. Seeing the holes in the car door and blood, he realized the man had been shot. Seeing he was pinned in the seat by the steering wheel, he tried to free him from the seat belt and the steering wheel with the help of others now on the scene.

A fire truck from the airport station arrived and started helping in the effort to remove the man. Two firemen started to assist the woman who was bleeding from her neck and arm. They placed a bandage on the neck wound, placed a brace on her to keep her from turning her neck and placed her on a stretcher, and covered her with a blanket.

***

Chapter 4

O ther firemen helped to remove the man from the car and were able to get the steering wheel off his legs and pull him out. Seeing he had several gunshot wounds and an extremely low pulse, the Fire Chief asked, "How far out are the paramedics?", to one of the other firemen standing near-by.

"About a minute, I can hear the sirens," one replied, while looking at the scene.

"We need to get them both to the hospital ASAP or they are not going to make it. I'm not sure he can wait much longer with the loss of blood he has," the chief said, looking at the man's wounds. You could hear ambulance sirens and see the lights in the distance, as other police officers now arriving were directing traffic from around the scene. As they arrived, they started to take control of the rubberneckers and nosey people who were slowing down to see what happened. The police were trying to get rubberneckers to keep moving and get traffic moving.

As two ambulances pulled onto the scene, the police cleared a path for the paramedics and firemen. The first paramedic started to prepare the woman and the second started working on the man to transport them to the hospital. The first ambulance took the woman, and the second took the man, leaving the scene of the shooting with sirens and lights at high speed both headed to San Francisco General Hospital.

The ambulance driver was talking to the hospital telling them they were inbound with a black female with gunshot wounds to the neck and arm and possible head trauma. "Yes, we have started an IV and she has a weak pulse; she is semi-conscious".

The two paramedics in the back were working on the IV and trying to get the bleeding to stop. One applied a lot of pressure to her arm and stuffed it with gauze. While the other wrapped a towel around her neck trying to keep it from moving, telling the driver to "step on it."

A B Hudson

The second ambulance driver was talking to someone at the hospital. "Inbound with a black male with multiple gunshot wounds, one to the left side of face, upper chest and back, possible leg injuries."

In the back, two paramedics were working hard to stop the blood from the wounds. One started an IV and placed a towel around the man's face to try to apply pressure to hold his mouth closed and attempting to stop the bleeding, while the other one was working on the wounds to his chest and arm.

"You better step on it or he is not going to make it", he said to the driver as he was holding the blood-soaked towel, replacing it with a clean one to the man's face. He was unconscious and his blood pressure was extremely low. He was breathing but he could barely feel a pulse. Blood was coming out of the other wounds, so he plugged them with gauzes and applied pressure to his chest and back.

The driver hit the gas and said to himself, *"I have not lost a person in two months and I'll be damn if I lose this one"*, pressing the gas pedal to the floor and guiding the truck through the street.

***

"This is Michael Black, KUTV channel 2, reporting from San Francisco airport. Two people were shot here just minutes ago, in what appears to be a drive by shooting. A couple leaving the airport were gunned down on the exit road. Airport police have not released the names of the victims. To my right is their car riddled with bullets while it slammed into the light pole.

Both victims a black male and woman were removed from the vehicle and are being transported to the trauma center at San Francisco General. We have no word as to their condition. Stay tuned for more information. This is Michael Black, reporting for KUTV Channel 2 news. Back to you in the studio Chris.

***

Chapter 5

Both ambulances arrived at San Francisco General Hospital pulling into the emergency parking spaces next to each other. The paramedic jumped out and shouted, "Black female with gunshot to the back of the neck, and arm, vital signs 110 /60 temp 102.2," as he pushed Nina into the emergency room.

Dr. Beaker, the doctor on duty in the emergency room, ran up to the gurney, along with a couple of nurses. Looking at Nina, Dr. Beaker was examining her while they pushed her into the emergency operating room. He was walking and talking .

"Let's get some pressure on her wounds and get her typed and in the OR now."

As a nurse started to type her the doctor said, "get me a clamp for this neck wound.

"Nurse, put some pressure on that wound." He barked orders.

"Start typing her for blood." The OR nurse said to the other nurse.

"Yes mam," the nurse said, and started drawing her blood as they pushed her into the emergency O.R.

***

They had not gotten to the operating room door before the second paramedic was pushing through the double doors. The second paramedic shouted coming through the door, "Black male, multiple gunshot wounds, one to the face, two in the back, two in the arm and one in the hand, vitals 129/65 Temp 101.1," as he pushed Nicholas into the emergency OR surgery.

The emergency room front desk nurse picked up the house intercom and paged the other emergency room doctor to the ER.

"Calling Dr. Chin, code blue, emergency room." "Code blue, emergency room," could be heard over the hospital intercom. Within a few seconds out of a set of double doors to the left of the

11

emergency room desk ran a short Chinese man, who looked to be no more than five feet two. He looked like a little boy playing doctor, the white coat he was wearing didn't seem to fit him. He had a round boyish face without any hair. His hair was cut close and he had a pair of horn-rimmed glasses that were perched on the end of his nose.

"What do we have here, he said to himself, more than to anyone around.

Dr. Chin, with his horn-rimmed glasses perched on his nose and sleep in his eyes, looked at the man on the gurney and immediately started to examine him.

"Move it people, get him in the OR now, and someone type him. I need a clean gown and gloves now, please," he said, as he was trying to plug the hole in Nicholas shoulder with his finger.

"Let's start to type him for blood," the nurse said, and turned to another nurse holding the IV bag, while the paramedic was holding the oxygen tank, as he pushed the man towards the operating room.

"Put some pressure on that wound", Dr. Chin said, as he was handed a clean gown and some gloves. As he slipped into the clean gown and gloves, he was still barking orders to the nurse.

Referring to one of the shoulder wounds, he wanted the nurse to put pressure on it, as they rolled him into the operating room.

The first paramedics came out of the operating room pushing his blood-soaked gurney. He started to clean the gurney replacing the bloody sheet with a clean one from the supply room. After he cleaned the gurney, he removed the latex gloves, placing them in the disposable can.

He approached the emergency room front desk. Taking the victim's personal property from under the gurney, he handed the nurse the personal property bag along with his company paper work. The desk nurse took the paperwork and the brown bag. She placed the bag in the property box under her desk. Then turning her attention to the paperwork in her hand, and thought, *"Let's see what we have?",* looking at him, she suddenly asked.

"Hey Andrew, you have a name for her?"

"No, we didn't have time, too busy getting here." He headed towards the exit.

"Check with James he may have some information." Andrew didn't care much for the old lady behind the desk, as she was dirty and treated people who came into the ER, as if they were dirt. He had seen her tell an old sick lady that a doctor could not see her because she didn't have any money. Knowing that she didn't have the right to refuse service to anyone. Fact of the matter was he just didn't like mean people. She was just mean and dirty.

"Oh, that's okay, I will just get it from her personal property."

***

The emergency room nurse went through Nina's personal things. She looked in her purse, finding her wallet, she determined her name was Nina Simmons from her driver's license. From her address book, she found information written in the space for emergency personal information, the name Maria Sanchez, with a phone number.

Writing the name Maria Sanchez and her number down on her pad. Taking Nina's sapphire and diamond pinky ring out of her purse, placing it in her desk drawer and looking around the area to see if anyone noticed her removing the ring. She saw no one was looking so she took the ring out of her desk drawer and placed it on her finger. It looked so nice. She held it under the desk and looked at it for a moment. Then thought, what else could she take?

***

Returning to Nina's purse she took out the money that was in it and put it in her purse under the desk. All said and done, she had robbed Nina of her money and ring, and was thinking about the man's bag which she had not gone through yet.

She then turned her attention to calling the next of kin and family. Picking up the phone she dialed the number on her pad.

***

Maria answered on the third ring, "Hello."

"Hello! Is this Maria Sanchez?", the nurse asked.

"Yes, it is," Maria replied, with a puzzled reflection on her face and some concern in her voice.

"I'm the emergency room nurse, at San Francisco General Hospital, calling on behalf of Nina Simmons. Do you know Nina Simmons? "The nurse asked, in a calm voice.

"Yes, I know Nina Simmons, what is the problem? Maria replied, with a lot more concern in her voice.

"She was brought into the emergency room; she has been in an accident. I'm trying to reach her next of kin," the nurse replied.

"Oh my God, I will be right there, is she okay? Maria said, and started to rush around the room. She hung up the phone without saying good-bye. She started to pray to herself.

"Oh my God, please God let her be okay," she said, grabbing her purse, coat and keys and headed out the door.

"Please let her be okay," Maria kept saying while she drove towards the hospital.

***

The second paramedic came out of the operating room pushing his blood-soaked gurney. He also began to clean his gurney, replacing the bloody sheet with a clean one from the supply room, and removed his latex gloves, placing them in the disposable can. His partner prepared to give the nurse the personal property belonging to the male victim.

He waited at the window for the emergency nurse to finish talking to an old man who had walked up to the other window and asked to see a doctor.

***

"Do you have insurance or are you on Medicare?", she asked the old man, who if one looked could see he was in a great deal of pain. However, that didn't mean a thing to her, she was going to get an answer to her question, or he was not going to see the doctor. The old man handed her what looked to be a small card, which turned out to be his Medicare card. He was in great pain and could barely stand there while she put him through the bullshit.

"Take a seat and your name will be called when someone is available to see you," she said, with an attitude that really said, get out of my face and closed the window.

***

Sliding her chair around to the window were the paramedic was standing, holding the male victim's personal property, she opened the window, taking the bag from the paramedic and placing it in the box under her desk.

Then she turned her attention to the paperwork he handed her. She looked at it and got heated again, because the driver had not put the name of the victim on the paperwork.

"Why did you not put the name of the person on the damn paperwork? I get tired of hunting for names and information that should be done before it gets to me," she said under her breath.

She was lazy and didn't want to do any more than she had to. Always looking for a way to get over, or to get out of doing any work at all. She had been a nurse for over twenty years and had not gotten ahead because of her laziness and attitude. Most of the other nurse's didn't talk to her if they didn't have to. Her own husband had left, because of the way she acted, which was lazy, and a genuine fat asshole. She had been a nice-looking woman back in the day, but she had let herself go, and now she was just bitter and mean.

***

After taking the bag and talking to the driver for a moment, he let her know he was not the one to be messed with, he had told her before that he didn't like her; and he would beat the shit out of her, if she came at him like he was a child. By the look in his eyes, she believed him and didn't have a lot to say to his face. Oh, but she talked about his ass as if he were a dog when he could not hear her. Facts be told, she liked him and wanted to see what he had going on, but with her weight, and the fact that she was a few years older than him, she knew she did not stand a chance.

***

Chapter 7

Turning her attention to the box under her desk, which had the male's personal belongings, she found a gold money clip holding two thousand four hundred dollars. Seeing it noted on the work sheet the drivers had handed her, she placed it back in the bag. Then opening the wallet, she found Nicholas driver's license, and fourteen one hundred-dollar bills, tacked behind a fold and a couple of credit cards.

She found a piece of paper with the name Tyrone on it and a phone number. She wrote down all the items in the wallet. However, the temptation was too great; she removed ten one hundred-dollar bills from the wallet, before placing it back in the bag.

Before she dialed the number she found, she placed the thousand dollars she had taken into her purse, under the desk, closed it, and thought about the new things she was going to buy. Then once again greed caused her to think, "if he died, how she would get the rest of the money in the wallet, as no one knew it was there in the first place." The paramedic didn't go through the bag and they had not seen the money tacked under the folder.

***

Interrupting her daydream, a young woman walked up to the window and asked to see a doctor with a great deal of stress and concern in her voice. "Hello, would you please help me... My daughter needs a doctor... She swallowed something, and she's turning blue. I need a doctor... I need to see the doctor, please let me see the doctor." The hysterical woman was saying over and over, while pleading with her eyes.

The emergency room nurse looked at her with no compassion or remorse whatso ever, showing no concern. While not even looking at the child, or the young mother, stated, "sign your name and have a seat, someone will be with you in a moment," said the nurse with a fake grin on her face, while handing the woman a tablet and a pen.

Holding the child, in her one arm and using the other arm, the young mother signed her name on the tablet and handed it back to the nurse and threw it in the hole in the security glass.

Once again sliding her chair, too lazy to get up, she looked at the name on the tablet and called for a practitioner to come to the emergency room. Reluctantly she summoned the woman back to the window and took her information and insurance cards and co-pay.

Showing no real concern for the woman or her child, she filled out the paper work and then told the young mother to wait in the waiting room for someone to call her name. Not once did the nurse ask how her child was or offer to aid her.

The young woman wanted to kick her ass, and if it were not for the fact that her daughter needed her, she would have. It was a good thing that the hospital had built a plastic cubicle with windows around the desk area or a lot of people may have jumped on this woman over the years.

***

She dialed the number she wrote down for Nicholas Simmons, on the second ring, a female picked up the phone.

"Hello, Vivian said, in a friendly voice.

"Hello, this is the emergency room nurse at San Francisco General Hospital," she replied.

"I'm calling trying to reach anyone at this number that may know a Nicholas Simmons. Have I reached a party that knows Mr. Simmons?" the nurse said.

"Yes, I know Mr. Simmons, what's wrong?" Vivian asked, with a sense of concern in her reply, making Tyrone sit up in his chair, trying to hear the conversation on the phone.

"Mr. Simmons was brought into the emergency room; he has been in an accident. I'm trying to notify his family that he is here, and that they need to come to the emergency room at San Francisco General Hospital, as soon as possible," she replied, with a calm smooth voice.

"Oh, my G, is he okay? What happened? Tyrone! Nickels is in the hospital, we have to get there now," said Vivian, not thinking about the nurse on the phone. Then realizing the nurse was still on the phone.

"What about Nina, was she with him?" Vivian asked the nurse with a great deal of panic in her voice.

The nurse replied, yes, she is also in the emergency room. In a state of panic Vivian hung up the phone, not realizing she hung up on the nurse. Turning towards Tyrone who was getting out of his chair, looking at her, with questions in his eyes. She just stood there not able to move or talk for a moment, and then she said, "We have to go," moving around the room in a state of panic and worried concern.

"That was a nurse at San Francisco General Hospital, she said, Nicholas and Nina were in an accident", stated Vivian to Tyrone, as she grabbed her coat and keys and started for the door. "We need to get to the hospital right away," she added while walking. Tyrone grabbed his coat and the two 9mm that sat next to him on the end table and was a half-step behind her. "Slow down and tell me that again", as they made their way to the garage. On the way, Vivian tried to slow down her thoughts and told him what the nurse had said to her.

Tyrone was wondering what Nicholas and Nina were doing in San Francisco in the first place. Nicholas was supposed to pick Nina up at the Oakland Airport. As he drove across the bridge, he was in deep thought; it was just how he processed information, always keeping his head on a swivel, looking for the unexpected around every corner.

* * *

Maria arrived at the hospital in less than fifteen minutes. Standing in front of the emergency room front desk, talking to the nurse, she was trying her best to stay calm, and get an understanding of what happened. However, the nurse was not giving her any information, which frustrated Maria to the point she wanted to slap the nurse.

"I'm sorry, but you will have to wait for the doctor. I'm not allowed to give information about patient's, only a doctor can speak on a patient's condition," the nurse said, with no sign of sympathy or concern on her face or in her voice.

"Well, can you tell me if they are alive or dead?", Maria said, with a lot of attitude.

"Miss, I'm sorry, but you have to wait for the doctor," the nurse said.

"That's fucked up!", Maria said, out of frustration and marched off to the waiting room.

She thought, *"Oh hell, I need to call Vivian, and let her know Nina and Nicholas are in the hospital,"* she had forgotten to call them from home. She looked in her purse and found the number Vivian had given her some time back.

***

Chapter 8

Detective Charles Moore a twenty-year veteran of the San Francisco Police Department and his partner, Detective Michael Thomas, an eighteen-year veteran, working homicide for the past 10 years, arrived at the scene of the shooting and walked over to the car. Looking at the bullet holes in the doors, and how the car was wrapped around the base of the light pole, they both wondered to themselves how the shooting went down.

As he looked at the holes in the driver's side and the broken windows Detective Moore thought to himself, *"Let's see, what do we have here?"*

Seeing no body bags, Moore was wondering why he got the call in the first place. However, with the Chinatown murders fresh in the media, he understood the dilemma the department was undergoing. Given all his years of experience, and his own instincts, he didn't believe this was a drug related incident.

The fact that he didn't know who this car belonged to... He thought he knew all the major dealers in the city and their cars. This one was new, and he could not place a name to it. Moore was not sure what to make of the scene.

Looking inside he saw all the blood and the flowers laying on the floor. The broken glass over the seats and the steering wheel busted. He looked at the back seat and saw that no one had been in the back. He took out his note pad and began to write in it. He took down the license number and the VIN number off the window.

Meanwhile his partner, Detective Michael Thomas, walked out into the street, which they had roped off. Taking out his own notepad, he began jotting down notes from the ground. Looking at the tire marks left by the van, he walked over to the officers and asked who was first on the scene. The officer who made the call walked over and started to tell him.

"Tell me... officer, what happened here?"

"I was on the way to report for duty, when I heard what sounded like a series of shots coming from some type of automatic gun. I then saw a black van on this side of the road headed toward the exit. I could not see who was firing, but I made a U-turn. By the time I was able to make the turn the van was gone. I called it in and started to help get the people over there out of the car. When the others arrived, I helped rope off the scene. Meanwhile, the crime scene tech people were gathering evidence and information for their reports."

***

Detective Moore and Thomas started to question the witnesses that they saw at the crime scene, and got an ID of the Van, but no one got the license number. All of them saw a black cargo van.

The man who helped get the woman out the car stated that he saw a white man driving and thought there may have been two or three people in the back. But he could not ID them. The officer who made the call stated, he saw the van headed south, but was busy trying to help get the man out the caddy.

***

The crime scene boys were collecting anything they could find. Thomas then walked back to the police car, where the man who first stopped to help was sitting. He had helped get the victims out of the car, and was an eyewitness to the shooting, and got a look at the people in the van. Once Thomas got to the police car, he took the report from the questioning officer, and took a glance at the initial reports taken from witnesses by the officers on the scene.

The man who pulled Nina and Nicholas from the car said that he hadn't got the license plate, but that the color of the van was black.

As he walked around the crime scene, Moore said," which hospital did they take them?", as he headed to his car.

"They were both taken to General," said the officer in charge.

The crime scene tech walked up to Moore and asked, "Can we tow this one?"

Nicholas II A Storm is Coming
"Yeah, go ahead and tow it," Moore told the tech.

Detectives Moore and Thomas headed to the hospital, leaving the crime scene techs to finish processing the crime scene. It puzzled them a couple leaving the airport was targeted, Moore wanted answers.

***

Maria looked around for the phone booths, spotting the phone booths down the hall she started walking towards them. She had just reached the phone booth, when Tyrone burst through the door of the emergency room, with so much bass in his voice, that it could have raised the dead, as he walked to the front desk, with Vivian right behind him.

"I want to know where Nicholas and Nina Simmons are," his voice seemed to make the walls vibrate.

"Sir, you have to lower your voice, and calm down", the nurse stated.

"Fuck calm, I want to know where they are," he said, just as loud and with a great deal of attitude.

The nurse looked down at the screen on her desk, and said, "Mr. Simmons and Mrs. Simmons are in surgery, sir, you have to calm down, or I will have to call for security. Please wait in the waiting room for the doctor to come out," the nurse stated, trying her best to get out of harm's way.

This fool standing here didn't look like he was going to be calm. She realized that the window she was behind was not going to stop this man if he wanted to reach her. Just as she was about to call for the police, a woman walked up and started to talk to him.

Vivian ran up to Tyrone trying to calm him down, she told him to chill, he was drawing too much attention to himself.

"Tee, Baby, calm down or they are going to call security," she said, in an effort to get him to lower his voice. Vivian was just about the only person, who could get this big ass nigger to chill, he was putty in her hands. However, to most others, he was bad news.

***

Nicholas II A Storm is Coming

Vivian spotted Maria walking toward them and started walking toward her. Maria raised her hand to draw attention from Vivian. Vivian saw Maria's raised hand and they met in the hallway and hugged.

"Hi, I was just trying to call you. When I got here, they would not tell me anything. All I know is they were in an accident of some kind. They are both in surgery and the doctors have not come out," looking over at the nurse with hate in her eye, "and that fucking nurse hasn't said shit," Maria said through threatening and tearful eyes.

Tyrone looked around and thought he had better chill, so he went to the waiting room and sat down. Then like a big cat caught by surprise he jumped to his feet, telling Vivian he had to go back to the car.

He forgot he had two 9mm's tacked in the small of his back. He was just about out the emergency room doors, when two cops Detectives Moore and Thomas walked in. They passed each other at the door but did not notice Tyrone.

Tyrone made it to the car, placed the 9mms in the glove box, locking it, and returned to the waiting room. The nurse thought to herself that she was lucky he didn't see her take the money. She was still thinking about the money and the fact that she wanted the rest before her shift was over. She didn't see or hear the police officers walk up to the window.

"You have two gunshot victims brought in from the airport, I'm Detective Moore and this is my partner Thomas, we need to see the personal property for both of them," said Moore, as he placed his badge on the glass, showing his picture and shield.

"Could you give us an update of their status?", asked Thomas, while showing his shield and picture.

"No, I don't have an update at this time, they are both still in the OR," she said, trying to look both of them in the eyes, but having a difficult time doing it. She then turned to the screen on the desk trying to avoid any eye contact with them.

"May we see the personal items that they had on them when they were brought in?", asked Moore, with a business-like voice.

"Yes officer, I have them here, you have to sign for them. You can use that office over there." Handing him the two bags and pointing them to the office, she was a little on edge about the money she took.

"Okay, let us know if the doctor comes out before we finish looking at this stuff please," Moore said to the nurse, and then walked to the office and closed the door.

After they had gone through everything in the bags, they made a note of the amount of money, putting everything back in the bags and gave both bags back to the nurse. They asked the nurse again, "has the doctor come out?"

"No officers, they have not come out yet", the nurse replied.

"Please have the doctor call me the moment he is out of surgery," he said, handing her his card.

Seeing that he could not get any more information from the nurse and guessing it would be some time before they would be able to talk to the victims, he decided that they would check on other things.

"Let's go check out the car, and try to piece this together," Moore said to his partner.

His partner meanwhile kept looking at the big man in the waiting room. He did not know where he knew him from, but something about him was awfully familiar. He just did not look the type that would be hanging around an emergency room at 9 o'clock at night. However, he just couldn't put a name to the face.

"Hey, you see that big guy over there in the waiting room?", he asked Moore, pointing with his head and eyes towards Tyrone.

"Yes, what about him," Moore shot back while glancing at the man.

"He just doesn't fit," replied Thomas, while trying his best to remember where or when he had seen the big man before.

"Okay, so do you know him? Is he wanted or something?", asked Moore, while walking toward their car in the parking lot.

"Not sure, I just get a gut feeling I have seen him before, that's all," Thomas stated, while walking and still trying to put a name or place to the face.

"Well, we have other fish to fry now, so let's get moving, I want to get home and get some sleep," Moore said, getting in the car to leave.

***

Chapter 10

The Simmons had in fact been coming from the airport, because they found suitcases in the trunk, and roses all over the front seat and floor. The driver's window was shot out and there were several bullet holes in the driver's door and numerous in the rear door. They found several bullet holes in the dash, some in the front driver's seat, and the center armrest covered with blood. The passenger window was broken, it could have been a bullet, or someone broke it to get Nina out, he believed it was most likely a bullet.

Moore walked around the car and thought to himself, "*Was this a missed hit? Did the Cadillac look like some other person's car? Or on the other hand, some type of hate crime. Maybe they just happened to be in the wrong place.*"

Moore had a lot of questions and no answers. Thomas was still struggling with where he knew that big dude in the emergency room from. He just could not put a name to the face. As they finished looking at the car, they decided to head back to the precinct and call it a night.

***

Heading to the precinct, Thomas and Moore rode in silence thinking to themselves. Moore reached in his jacket pocket and took out a pack of camels and lit a cigarette and blew the smoke towards the roof of their crown Vic and said, "I don't know what happened back there but it sure looks like someone tried to take them out," lowing a cloud of smoke towards the window.

"Yeah, looks like the man could have been the mark, the woman got hit when they sprayed the car," Thomas said, while looking out the windshield at the storm clouds gathering over the bay.

"We need to talk to them if they make it out of surgery. We may be able to shed some light as to why, or maybe even who, pulled the trigger," Moore said, and continued to enjoy his cigarette. "It's almost one and I need to get home and get some rest, this case is not going anywhere. The Lab will not have a report until this afternoon, and we don't have any bodies," Thomas said, and looked at Moore for confirmation.

"Okay, I need to go and get some rest also," he stated, as he pulled into a parking spot at the precinct and cut the engine. After locking the shotgun rack, and turning off the radio, they both got out and locked the car.

***

Inside the precinct, they went to their office on the third floor and both flopped down in the office chairs facing each other. Moore looked at the phone and saw that he had a missed called. He thought about checking the messages but decided that they could wait. His mind was tired, and his body was in bad need of water and rest. He got up, told his partner good bye, and headed to the garage to get his car.

Thomas was still trying to put a name to the face of the man he saw at the hospital. He knew he had seen him before but could not place him. He thought about going through some mug shots, but his body and mind were telling him, he too, needed to let it go and get some rest. He pushed back from the desk and stood up, walked to the garage, got in his mustang, and headed home.

***

D rake and Carmella laid exhausted in the bed while listening to jazz. Drake sat up and turned on the television, just in time to hear the reporter talking about a shooting at the airport. He looked at the screen and wondered who was it that got shot.

He and Carmella were still nude, sweating from their love making session. He was not ready to handle the fine ass Colombian for a third round. So, he pulled the sheet from around his legs and got out the bed and looked at the screen on the wall.

Carmella was watching the screen from the bed, she got up and let the sheet fall from her body, allowing her sweaty sexy body, to shine in the light of the fireplace. She headed toward the bathroom. Play time was over, she needed to know for sure that Nicholas was dead.

"Well, you sure as hell can't go like that", Drake said, looking at her fine ass as she walked towards the bathroom. She looked back over her shoulder and smiled a devilish smile while she thought, "I should just shoot you now and take your shit, but the dick is good, and I can use a break."

 While Drake was watching the news, Carmella took a shower and dressed, then walked out the bathroom, and headed downstairs to the living room. Drake followed her down, wearing a pair of basketball shorts and a wife beater. He was still processing the fact that the news was reporting the shooting of Nicholas, a businessman from Oakland, at the airport this evening. Drake knew that Nicholas was a great deal more than a businessman. Nicholas was the head of the Mexican Cartel, and a Kingpin in the drug game.

Drake was aware that the shooting was going to bring a shit storm of trouble and pain for a lot of people. Tyrone would be out for blood and he was not one to be taken lightly.

Nicholas II A Storm is Coming

"What... you going to come here, fuck me, and just get up and walk out," said Drake to Carmella, with a smile on his face. He knew he had laid the pipe to her right.

"No papa... I'm not that kind of girl. I have to handle some business that can't wait. You understand, I'm a businesswoman, and just like you I have to keep my head in the game. Believe me, this shooting is something I have to check on right away. So, forgive me if I hurt your feelings, I'll make it up tonight, if you let me, but right now I have to go," replied Carmella, as she headed to the door.

Carmella got in her car that was parked in the driveway of Green's house and picked up the phone. She called the hotel, ring...ring...ring... A voice answered on the third ring, "Hello, oh hey boss"

"What's going on? Did they get him? Is he dead?", asked Carmella, with a great deal of concern in her voice.

"Oh yeah, they got him at the airport... But I don't know if he's dead. The report I got was they were both taken to the hospital," replied the bodyguard.

"Are you sure they got him?", asked Carmella again, getting mad and wanting to slap the shit out of her bodyguard for being so dumb.

"Oh yeah, they loaded up the caddy with him in it, got his bitch also."

"But is he dead, any of you fools think to check the hospitals?", asked Carmella, in a deadly voice.

"I was just getting ready to, before you called," replied the guard, in his defense.

"Well, you have talked to me, now get your ass up and find out if he is gone!"

"I'm on it boss."

Carmella didn't wait to hear what he said, she hung the phone up.

Her plan was coming together, and she didn't want it to fall apart now.

Before leaving Drake, she had told him "I will call you in the morning, and let you know when and where you can get the package, and how to set up the drops for the next month." Now walking to her car, she was wondering if she would be able to take over the whole west coast.

Her driver was sitting in the car waiting. She knew he would not leave while she was in the house. If he thought she was in any trouble, he would run through hell wearing gasoline draws for her. He was her lover and friend as well as her bodyguard. But unless she was in trouble, he would just wait outside in the car, while she handled her business.

" Let's get to the hotel, she said, as she got comfortable in the back seat.

"Are you okay boss," he asked.

"Yes, I'm fine, that matter has been taken care of."

"That's good."

"Yes, that is good news for me, bad news for Drake Green."

"You want me to take him out now?" he asked, with a sound of hope in his voice.

"No, not yet, I still have a use for him," she said, and looked out the window, while the driver headed towards her hotel.

***

Chapter 12

When they arrived at the hospital, they were told to wait in that sterile disinfectant smelling waiting room, with that sanitation smell that only hospitals seem to have. Vivian was shocked to see all the people sitting there crying and in pain waiting to be seen by a doctor.

Two hours later, nervous, and anxious, jumping to their feet every time any person wearing a white coat and looking like a doctor passed, or someone called a name for treatment.

It was just after 1:30 am when a doctor walked out the double doors marked *"Emergency Personnel Only"*, and asked, "Is the family of Nina Simmons here?", while looking around the waiting room.

He was a tall skinny man, wearing a clean pair of scrubs. He looked to be in his mid-forties, with a 5 o'clock shadow. They all stood up together and replied, "yes, we are here for Nina Simmons."

He walked over to them, "I'm Dr. Becker, and I just finished surgery on Mrs. Simmons. We repaired the damage the bullet to her neck caused and stabilized her with a neck brace to prevent any movement. We removed the bullet that was lodged in her arm and put in seven stitches to close the wound in her hand, where a bullet passed through."

"**What bullet**! We thought she was in a car accident. You saying she was shot?" Vivian said, with a lot of attitude, cutting him off in midsentence.

"Yes, she was in a car accident and also, she was shot; however, I expect her to fully recover in a few weeks. I have prescribed a sedative and medication that will aid in her healing," he said, trying to calm Vivian down and then he continued.

"She is going to have to get lots of rest. She is on her way to recovery now and in a couple of hours, you should be able to see her. I'm going to be monitoring her neck wound and keep it immobilized for a day or two," he said, trying to look at each of them as he spoke .

"Thank you, Doctor, when did you say we can go and see her?", Maria asked, looking the doctor in the eyes. While not really hearing what he was saying because she was into her feelings and thinking about her friend. She was praying and talking at the same time.

"You are welcome, when she comes out of recovery and the nurses have her in a room, I will have the nurse come get you," he said, as he turned to walk away.

"She was shot," Tyrone said, more to himself than to anyone, looking for confirmation from the doctor.

"Yes, she was shot in the neck and arm. One bullet passed through the back of her neck just missing a major artery, a few centimeters to the left and she would have bled out within minutes. She was lucky it missed," Dr. Becker stated.

JR and Devon, his brother, were standing there listening to the doctor and thinking to themselves. "What the hell was going on? Their father and stepmother were not out in the streets any longer, so who would want to shoot them?"

***

JR was wondering, who and why. He had heard stories about a man named Drake Green from the city, but from what he knew, that could not have been Drake. He was at war with the Chinese. The longer he thought about it the madder he got. His brother Devon was just standing there looking at the doctor like he was in some type of weird dream. He was trying to process the whole thing and yet it felt unreal.

Tyrone was getting furious, as he thought, *"who in the hell shot her,"* to himself. Then turned and asked the doctor, "what about Nickels, did he get shot also?", asked Tyrone with a seriousness in his voice, which caused the doctor to look at him.

"Who," the doctor asked, not recognizing the name Nickels.

"Mr. Simmons, did he get shot also?" asked Tyrone again, this time with a strained voice.

Nicholas II A Storm is Coming

"I cannot speak about Mr. Simmons, I was treating Mrs. Simmons," the doctor stated, as he looked down at the chart in his hand. He read something in the chart and then stated, "I believe Dr. Chin treated Mr. Simmons. When he is finished in surgery, I'm sure he will speak to you; now if you would excuse me, I have to look in on Mrs. Simmons", he stated, and walked away.

***

Tyrone stood there while Doctor Becker was talking, getting hotter by the minute. *"What the fuck is he talking about she was shot, who shot her, and what was going on?"* He needed to make some moves. Nick was supposedly only in the city to pick up Nina from the airport.

Tyrone wanted answers and he wanted them now.

He knew he had to protect the women, making sure nothing happened to them, he could not be slipping. He got up, went to the phone booth, and called Roland and Charles. He told Roland to get four men over to the hospital to guard Nick and Nina. Telling him to make sure they had licenses to carry. He told Charles to call the rest of the crew and shut down. He instructed Charles to find out what was happening in the streets, who was talking, and what they were saying? He wanted answers and he wanted them quickly.

He told them both not to divulge to anyone where Nicholas and Nina were, or to let anyone know they were alive. He then turned toward Nicholas' two sons and said, "look here, we need to get our people out in the streets fast and find the ones who did this. I don't know who did it or ordered it, but we are going to find them, bet that" said Tyrone, with a great deal of confidence.

"Hey uncle, you know we don't have a lot of connections in the city, or people we can reach out to," said Devon, with a strange look in his eyes; like how we going to find them without becoming a target ourselves?

"We have enough, put a price of ten thousand on the street, snitches will come for that type of bread. Trust me, we're going to get them, I will be damned if we let this go. I will raise the dead if I have to," said

Tyrone, with eyes that seemed to be piercing into a person's soul. They stood there in the corner of the ER talking for a few more moments then Tyrone told them to head home, and that he would call them when something new happened.

Vivian knew the moment the doctor said "shot" she was not going to be able to control or hold Tyrone back. She knew her man, and knew he was the monster that some said he was.

Most people believed he needed to be chained behind a glass wall with a sign that warned, *"Break only in case of war."* She realized someone or thing had just broke the glass and unchained the monster. They didn't realize they had released a monster, and once released you cannot unbreak the glass. He was now moving towards monster mode and the streets were going to feel the pain.

It had been four years ago since the last time he went off. Fourteen people lost their lives, he killed dogs and any other pets, and he burned down houses.

Sitting in their office going over the latest information they had about Nicholas Simmons and the crime family he ran; Special agents Donald McDowell and Eric Gomez were set to start their investigation into Nicholas. They had been trying to make a case for the past five years on Nicholas.

However, they had always fallen short of getting any Indictments. Not enough evidence, or their CI came up dead or missing. Witnesses, all of a sudden changed their testimony, or lost their memory, or just came up missing. Donald sat at his desk and thought was this going to be the day they got a break and finally nail Nicholas.

***

Chapter 13

Coming out of the Green Lite club on Market, P-Slim walked up to the little black skin ho standing on the corner trying to catch a trick, "say bitch, where the fuck you been for the past thirty minutes," shouted P-Slim at the ho, as he walked up to her.

"Hey daddy, you know I was on my game, I had this trick in the alley and he wanted more of my time. So, I charged him like you told me," replied the hoe, and said, "here." Handing him two hundred dollars in twenty's.

He looked at her and told her, "now get your ass back out there and get my money. What you think, I have time to wait for you, now get out my face," said P-Slim while turning around and heading back in the bar.

Dirty Mike, watching from the window, just shook his head, as P-Slim was pimping out in front of the bar. Dirty Mike smiled and turn around on the stool and took a sip on his beer. P-Slim walked back into the bar and took a seat next to Dirty Mike at the bar.

"If that bitch doesn't have my money right by the time I finish this beer, I'm gonna put my foot in her ass, believe that," stated P-Slim in his best pimp voice.

"Well, you know the bitch ain't been right since that trick pulled a knife on her the other day," replied dirty Mike.

"Yeah, that shit was fucked up, but I don't care about him pulling a knife. I don't give a damn about any of that shit. She needs to get my money, said P-Slim with a little smile in the corner of his mouth.

"On a difference subject," said Dirty Mike, with a serious tone in his voice.

What are you planning to do about that dude William over in the city? And what about Oscar and Juan and those two Mexicans that were with him asking about Nicholas, asked dirty Mike, with a hint of concern in his voice.

"I don't plan to do nothing, guess they wanted to know, so I told them what they wanted to hear; that's all, no more, no less. We got paid and as far as I'm concerned, they can get their asses shot up by Nicholas and Tyrone," said P-Slim, trying to sound hard.

"P", "we are not in the same league as Nicholas and Tyrone, and I for one don't want them on my ass," said Dirty Mike, with a hint of fear in his answer.

"Hey fellows, can I get you something" asked the bartender, who was standing behind the bar with a smile on his face.

"No Jim, I'm done, I'm leaving... have some business I need to take care of; besides, I have to check my ho's and see what's cooking," said P-Slim, and got up to leave the bar.

"No... I need to get up out of here and check on that little bird I put on seventh street," said dirty Mike, as he turned to P-Slim and gave him a handshake and fist pound.

"See you at the locker in about an hour, or do you want to meet at the Game later tonight?", said P-Slim.

"I'll see you at the locker in about an hour, then we can go to the city and see what's shaking? Later my man," replied Dirty Mike.

As they walked out the bar, the bartender was thinking to himself, those two have got to be the biggest fuck up's in Oaktown." For they were always talking about ho's and money and never had any money and every ho they pulled someone took within a week. P-Slim had the looks, but not the brains to be a good pimp, he ran his mouth to much.

Now Dirty Mike was what the streets called a side man. A man who ran with someone else and lived off of the other man. Dirty mike had a ho that worked to pay him, she was in love. Mainly because he was the only one who would put up with her shit. So, he just hung with P-Slim and whatever they got into was fine with him. The bartender cleaned the area where they had sat and then turned to the next man at the bar and asked, "May I get you something?"

***

Nicholas II A Storm is Coming

Oscar and Juan got to the San Jose airport only to find that there were no flights out and the terminal was closed for the night. The schedule on the overhead screen showed the first flight in the morning was at 6:30 am, to Denver, with a connection to Houston. They would have to stay in town until morning, so they went to the Holiday Inn and got a single room with two queen size beds.

Sitting on the bed closest to the door, Oscar took the phone and placed a call to Houston.

Ring...Ring...Ring...

"Hello, talk to me," Flip said, while placing the phone to his ear.

"Hello, hey boss, it's me Oscar," replied Oscar, sounding upbeat.

"Yeah, what you got to tell me?", replied Flip.

"Our friend is gone, we got him at the airport about an hour and a half ago," said Oscar.

"Okay, glad to hear the news, when will I be seeing you?", Flip said, trying to talk in a code on the phone.

"We are stuck in San Jose for the night because there are no flights out. We are going to catch a plane in the morning and be in Houston by afternoon," said Oscar.

"I want you guy's out of there as fast as possible, so get on that first plane; keep out of site until then, understand?"

"Yeah, we are at the Holiday Inn, and don't plan on going anywhere, unless we go get something to eat, which I doubt we will go far."

"Don't go anywhere or let people see you, just hang until you get on that plane, understand?"

"Yes, I hear you; we burned the van and took a cab here, so I have covered our tracks."

"Don't think... I don't pay you to think... I pay you to do, now do what I said and stay put."

"Alright boss I hear you." "Not that it matters, but the room number here is 412."

"Okay, now get here fast as possible," said Flip, and hung up the phone before Oscar could say anything.

"What did Flip have to say", asked Juan, as he came out the bathroom and closed the door.

"Not a lot, he wants us to get there as fast as we can. Seems he thinks we are in trouble for not getting out of here tonight," said Oscar.

"Well did you tell him that there are no flights tonight," asked Juan.

"Yeah, I told him that and he just kept on talking about getting out of town."

"Well, we will be on the first plane in the morning, and in Houston by the afternoon. Did you tell him that?" asked Juan.

"Yeah, fool, I told you, he is just tripping. He told me not to leave this room to eat. He is simply scared and somewhat paranoid."

***

Meanwhile, back at San Francisco general Hospital, Dr. Chin was still in surgery, removing the bullets in Nickel's back. One had entered his back just below the left shoulder blade and traveled down toward the liver. It was the most urgent concern, Dr. Chin had to repair all the muscle and tissue where the bullet entered and traveled.

Another had entered his back just under his left rib, and one entered his back going through his right lung. Dr. Chin worked on him for over four hours before he was able to get all the damage repaired. The bullets in his left arm were no major problem to remove and stitch up. The bullet that hit him in the mouth, taking out three teeth on the left side and two on the right side of his lower jawbone, meant he was going have to undergo a lot of surgery on his jaw, if he survives this surgery.

***

All in all, Dr. Chin had been working for five and a half hours. Now two in the morning, he finished and left the operating room, washed his hands, changed into some clean scrubs, and headed to the waiting room. He was glad that he would be able to tell the family that their loved one was going to live. He hated to be the bearer of bad news.

He entered the waiting room, looked at the clock on the wall, seeing it was 2:23 am in the morning. "Is the family here for Mr. Simmons?" he asked.

With very sleepy eyes and tired backs, they jumped up from their chairs and answered the doctor.

"Yes, we are here for Mr. Simmons," Vivian replied, with Tyrone and JR jumping to their feet at the same time. Maria stood there with her hands in a praying position and prayed everything was fine.

"I have finished operating on Mr. Simmons and he has survived the operation. However, he is still in critically serious condition. We are moving him to the ICU for monitoring and observation. He will not be able to receive any visitors at this time, as we have placed him in a chemically induced coma, given his profoundly serious condition, and he is not out of danger. Therefore, I will be monitoring him every couple of hours," he said, as he looked around at them.

"When can we see him?", Maria asked, and looked at the Doctor with concern.

You may be able to look in on him later today; however, he will remain in a coma for a week or so to control movement, while his body heals," Dr. Chin explained, while looking at each of them.

"Doctor, you say he is in a chemically induced coma. Why did you put him in a coma"? Vivian asked, with concern on her face, as Tyrone looked on with concern. Maria just continued to pray and rock back and forth on her feet.

"Yes, he is, the bullets in his back were in bad places. We were able to remove them, but I cannot tell yet how well his body is going to react to the trauma the bullets caused to the nervous system. However, he looks to be in excellent physical condition and his signs are very encouraging. We will just have to wait and see how hard he fights," he said, trying to sound reassuring.

"Thank you, Doctor," they all responded, and looked at each other.

Maria continued to pray and cry to herself, while Vivian was trying to think of a way to hold Tyrone down, from going ape shit crazy and killing everything, and everybody he thought had anything to do with this. Tyrone was in his own world, gearing up for the storm clouds he saw on the horizon. The street was getting dark and ready for war.

***

They assigned Nina a private room on the fifth floor once she left recovery. It was almost three-forty-five in the morning, when a nurse from the emergency room walked into the waiting room of emergency and asked if the family of Nina
Simmons were there. The family members stood up and approached the nurse who was standing near the double doors. Vivian replied to her, "Yes, we are the family of Nina Simmons. Maria, JR, Devon, and

Tyrone stood there while the nurse told them they could go to the fifth floor, after which the nurse went back in the double doors leaving them standing there. They got their coats and headed to the elevators and got off on the fifth floor.

They walked up to the nurses' station and asked to see Mrs. Nina Simmons. The little Chinese nurse looked at her monitor and said that Mrs. Simmons is in room 534.

"Only two can go in at a time," she said, with a pleasant voice.

"You two go, and we'll wait here," Tyrone said.

"You can wait over there," the nurse said, pointing toward an area next to the nurses station.

"I'll just check on her, and then come out, so you can come back," Vivian said to Tyrone, then kissed him on the cheek. Maria and her then walked toward Nina's room, while JR, Devon and Tyrone walked to the waiting room and sat down.

***

Tyrone told JR to sit tight while he went to the phone booth to call Roland. He wanted a progress report from Roland, on where he stood on getting the men to guard Nina and Nicholas.

Beep...Beep...Beep, sounded the mobile phone in Roland's car. Picking it up and pressing the button to activate it," Roland said hello, talk to me, in a manly voice.

"Hey my man. How are you doing with getting the men I asked for? And how long before they are here?", asked Tyrone, with a concerned tone in his voice.

"Hey boss I'm almost there, I'm about five minutes away. I got six men licensed to carry and bonded. Where do you want to meet up at?", replied Roland.

"Good, now listen up...I need two men on the fifth floor and two in the ICU area. The other two will be outside the hospital. Meet me at the emergency room waiting room. I'll fill you in when you get here, so hurry," replied Tyrone, and hung up the phone and went back to the waiting area to join JR and Devon. He brought them up to speed on the men, and they talked about how they were going to handle the rest of the family.

Tyrone told JR he was going to set up a meeting with the rest of the family later in the morning; to start thinking about putting some protection around everyone in the family. He told Devon to start coming up with a plan detailing how they were to handle the product.

JR asked, "Uncle, are we going to tell the family where Nicholas and Nina are? You going to trust that information with everyone? Or are you going to keep that under wraps for the time?"

"I think we are going to keep it under the hat for the time. I want to look at their faces when I talk to them. So, for now, don't mention their whereabouts, they already know from the news, he was shot, so leave it like that for now. The truth is we don't know who to trust right now, or who we are looking for."

"Yeah, I agree, we need to play this close to the vest. The less people know the better," said Devon.

"Yeah, but has anyone called his Doctor? Doctor Logan, I know he would want his own doctor to be aware of his condition, said JR to the two of them.

"You are right, we need to get a hold of Doc Logan and get him here to look in on him," said Tyrone.

Tyrone got up and left again for the phone booth and called Doctor Logan, while JR and Devon talked.

"JR, do you think we need to call mom's and let her know about pop's?"

"No, I don't think that would be wise. Nicholas has moved on, and besides, mom's has her own life." "I did call and have a couple of my guy's sit on the house." They both smiled and continued their conversation as Tyrone approached them.

"I think we are going to move him just as soon as Doc says he is out of danger," said Tyrone, with concern in his voice. "Roland will be here in a few to set up security around them and Doctor Logan is on the way."

***

Chapter 15

The room was dark, the only sound heard was that of the machines. Nina was hooked up to some kind of hanging device, with tubes in her arm and nose, and a big ass brace on her neck, that held her head straight and stiff. Her face had a few small scratches with bandages, and her left eye was puffy and black and blue. Nina had bandages on her left arm, and she looked like she was in a great deal of physical pain and discomfort. However, the medicines were deeply influencing the pain, so while she looked uncomfortable, she was not feeling any pain.

Her hair was a mess, all over her head. Maria reached into her purse, taking out a comb and brush. She was going to comb Nina's hair, when Vivian said, "we better wait on combing her hair, until we find out how she is."

"I just don't want anyone to see her like that. You know damn well if she knew anyone saw her like this, she would blow it," Maria said, feeling sad, with tears in her eyes, as she looked at her best friend.

***

The sound of someone in the room caused Nina to try and open her eyes. She could not turn her head because of the neck brace. Because of the med's, she wasn't feeling any pain. She barely remembered the accident and shooting. She tried to talk but the words were coming extremely hard.

"Where is Nick?" she said, in a low whisper with a lot of concern.

"He is fine, he is okay, just lay back and rest, we're here," Maria said, and took hold of her right hand.

"Yes, he is doing fine, you just lay back and rest," Vivian said, and moved to where Nina could see her.

"I know it's a dumb question but how are you feeling?", she asked, and looked at her friend.

Nicholas II A Storm is Coming

"All I remember is we were leaving the airport, and Nick yelled duck!"

"Now just rest Nina," Maria and Vivian said together.

Nina felt the tears running down her cheeks and wanted to wipe them but couldn't. Her mouth was dry and sore, she wanted some water.

"Give me some water please," Nina said, with a weak voice.

"Vivian poured a little water from the pitcher on the tray and held it to her lips. Nina tried to suck the water through the straw, but it hurt to swallow.

"I'm going to try to comb your hair and fix you up a little, you look a mess," Maria said, and tried to smile.

"Do I look that bad?" Nina said, unable to raise her hands up to her head.

"Girl, you would whip your own ass if you could see how you look now," she said, and they all tried to smile.

They sat there looking at her and rubbing her arm and legs, for about ten minutes, before Vivian said, "Tyrone is out in the waiting area, I'm going out so he can come say Hi."

***

Tyrone walked into the room and was shocked to see Nina so messed up. He thought to himself, *"I'm going to fuck somebody up"*, as he moved toward her bed and leaned down and kissed her on the cheek and said, "Hey baby girl."

"Tyrone," Nina said, in a weak voice, barely audible for him to hear.

"It was a hit of some kind, they pulled up and started shooting."

"You have to get the car, there is a gun in the glovebox," she told him.

"Don't worry about any of that right now, you just get better; I'll worry about the car," he told her, but made a note to call the lawyer just as soon as he left her room.

The little Chinese nurse entered the room and told them," You will have to leave now. However, you may return during regular visiting hours. Mrs. Simmons needs her rest and her doctor wants to check on her," the nurse said, with a very sweet-sounding Asian accent.

***

Leaving the fifth floor, they headed back to the emergency room to check on Nicholas in the ICU. Dr. Chin had already told them they wouldn't be able to see him before they went up to Nina's room.

However, they were going to check on him anyway, to satisfy their curiosity and assure themselves Nicholas was safe, and the two guards were on duty. Also hoping that circumstances had changed for the better while they were up seeing about Nina.

Seeing that there was no change in his condition, they decided sitting around the hospital was not going to change the situation. They prepared to leave and started saying their good byes.

Vivian and Maria made plans to catch up later in the day, or if anything should change or happen. They exchanged numbers and gave each other a hug. Maria gave JR and Devon a hug and told them bye. Vivian walked over to Devon and JR and gave each a hug and kiss on the cheek. "Tell your mother hi for me when you talk to her. But I don't have to tell you not to tell her where Nicholas and Nina are," Vivian reminded them, while searching their eyes for confirmation that they understood. They both acknowledged their understanding. JR stated, "We got you aunt V." Devon didn't reply, he just nodded his head.

***

T hen "Did anyone call Dr. Logan and tell him that Nicholas and Nina were in the hospital?", Vivian asked, as she turned towards Devon who was now on the phone calling his younger brother.

Tyrone looked at her and replied that he had called Doctor Logan, when he called Roland and Charles, he would check with Roland and find out if they had seen him. He knew that Roland had gotten the men to guard both Nicholas and Nina's rooms and posted two men outside the hospital.

He was not taking any chances that whoever pulled this would be able to get in and finish the job. He was also going to move them out of San Francisco to some other place, safe, as fast as he could. However, with Nicholas in a coma, he had to wait for Doctor Logan to set up the move and let him know it was safe to move him.

As he was thinking, a tall white-haired man with a white coat walked out of the ICU room that Nicholas was in.

"Hello, Mr. Tyrone, how are you doing? I've just finished examining Mr. Simmons, and I concur with the attending doctor to leave him in a chemically induced coma. Thereby, allowing his body to heal and maintain the lowest amount of pain, allowing his body to fight off the trauma; at this moment; he is resting comfortably, and he has a morphine drip. I will check on him later this morning. Now with your permission, I am going up to examine Mrs. Simmons," said Dr. Logan, as he headed toward the elevators.

"Doctor Logan," "is there any way we could move Nicholas to a secure location with a safer environment, that we can control?", Tyrone asked.

Dr. Logan stopped and turned facing Tyrone. "Well, he is not out of the woods yet, but if everything goes well today, we may be able to move him to a secure location in a day or two."

"We don't have a day or two, whoever did this is going to try to get at him to finish the job, if they find out he is still here, do you

49

understand?", said Tyrone to Dr Logan, who was standing there thinking to himself. "Yes, I understand, but if I move him, I could cause him more harm. But he is right, whoever did this will try again." Slipping out of his thoughts, he replied to Tyrone, "You are right, I will make the arrangements and get him ready to move within the next six hours. I'll make arrangements to have everything set up, and I will hire the nurses to care and watch over him. I think I know the perfect hospital to use."

"I will leave it to you to make that happen, meanwhile, I'm gonna keep people here to watch over both of them," said Tyrone.

"Don't worry, he won't be in any danger, I'll be here," said Roland, from the doorway to Nicholas's room; while sitting in a chair with his arms folded across his chest, holding on to the two nines under his arm pits.

Only the Doctor and the Nurses are going in or out this room", said Roland, in a boss like voice.

"This is a good hospital with a very good trauma center," said Doctor Logan, he will be getting the best treatment possible here.

"That may be, but I still want our people to be here", said Tyrone.

"I fully understand," replied Doctor Logan, as he turned and walked toward the elevator.

"I'll give you a call just as soon as I have everything arranged", he said, to Tyrone, as he passed him.

***

JR knew he was going to have to think quick and to be on his p's and q's, for this was going to get messy. There was no telling where it would lead. He was thinking that if it were a hit, it could be any number of groups; the Italian mafia or Russian mafia, or even if the Mexican Cartel could be behind it.

Given the unprecedented move that Nicholas was trying to make, getting the family out of the drug game, and into legitimate business interests, it could be any number of people coming after Nicholas. Then again, it could be some nut case, some fool from the past who was trying to carry out a grudge. Either way, he was gonna have to step up his game.

JR now understood the saying his father use to tell him. "Every so often in this game, it comes a time when things just bust open. You know, like when you see the storm clouds gather and they get dark, the darker they get, the louder the thunder and lightning, and the harder it rains, when they finally release all the penned-up pressure in them;" Nicholas would tell him, when they were driving to Reno to ski. JR thought it was strange how he could recall little things his father had told him years ago.

"Yes", "A Storm was Coming", bad things were about to happen! The rain hasn't started, but the thunder had been sounded. Now the lightning was going to flash from the sky and dance across the ground. JR could feel the rain in the air, he can smell it, almost taste it. JR looked out the window of the hospital and said to himself, "The clouds keep gathering and getting darker, yes, a storm is coming." He then turned and walked back to the rest of the family.

***

Tyrone was in his own world. Tyrone was trying to figure out in his mind just who was coming at them. He walked toward the window and buried his head in his hands. He thought, *"Who has a problem with us that they would come like this?"* He was deep in thought when Vivian touched him, and said, "We need to get home and get some rest."

"Yeah, I need to get you home, so I can make some calls," he said, as he turned and looked down at her with wet tear-filled eyes; but she also saw a little of the cold hearted, evil killer in his eyes.

"They are going to be okay, don't worry baby," V said, and walked into his arms, placing a kiss on his cheek and then lips.

"Yeah, but I 'm going to kill whoever is behind this shit, believe that," he said, with a determination and hate in his voice she had never seen before and knew she didn't want to know.

Vivian and Tyrone said their good-byes and walked out the hospital doors to their new 85 Lincoln town car and drove home in silence.

***

Chapter 17

C BS News reported that the man and woman shot at the San Francisco International Airport last night were two very prominent citizens from Oakland, CA. Mr. Nicholas Simmons is President & CFO of Simmons Engineering, one of the largest black owned engineering firms in the country.

"Reporting from the San Francisco General Hospital, this is Mark Lowes, I'm standing here at the emergency room entrance. I spoke to a Dr. Douglas, Chief of Medicine, here at San Francisco General.

He released a statement that read, Mr. Simmons had several Injuries, and that Mr. Simmons was currently in ICU, in a coma. Mrs. Simmons had several injuries and she is currently in guarded condition. The San Francisco Police Department did not release any information, only stating this is an ongoing investigation.

Authorities were not releasing any other information about the shooting. No suspect was in custody and the San Francisco police ask, if you have any information, contact the San Francisco Police Department. Back to you Jean, Mark Lowes, reporting from San Francisco General."

***

Sitting at the counter eating some eggs, P-Slim looked at the TV mounted on the wall. The morning news was going on about the shooting at the airport. He looked at the screen and heard the reporter say Nicholas Simmons was still alive and in a coma. He almost choked on that bit of news. It would not be good for him if Nicholas lived. He was the one who fingered Nicholas to William Franklin for five-thousand dollars. He knew that if William got caught, he would snitch everyone out.

P-Slim listened to the news reporter and thought that he was going to have to get at William before he could talk to anyone. But, how could he? He didn't know where William lived and was pretty damn sure William would not be on the streets now.

Just as he was finishing his food, Dirty Mike, his partner, walked in, and asked if he had heard the news. P-Slim and Dirty Mike left the diner and headed to the hotel, where P-Slim lived. They were trying to think of a way to get out of the mess they found themselves in.

***

Carmella heard the news while she was drinking a cup of coffee, sitting on the sofa in her hotel. She jumped up and threw the cup across the room when the reporter said Nicholas was in a coma, and not dead. Rushing to the phone she dialed a number, and when the phone was answered, she said, "Hello, let me speak to the boss."

"Who is this?" said a voice, in a deep Mexican accent.

"Just say its Carmella and give the phone to your boss," said Carmella, in a disgusting voice.

"Hello, little one", said a voice, with a hint of sex in it.

"Hey, there has been a little problem here, they hit Nicholas last night, but they didn't kill the fuck."

"What the hell you mean they hit him and didn't kill him? I want that nigger dead, and I want it today!"

"Well, I thought the two you sent were good, but it looks like they fucked up. I will see what I can do before I have to get the fuck out of town myself. I will get back to you sometime today, and let you know what I can get done", said Carmella, and hung up the phone.

Just as soon as she hung up, she called her son in Houston and told him that she wanted him to kill Oscar and Juan. Her son Roberto was happy to hear the news that he could kill Oscar. He then put the word out to shoot them on sight. He also put a five-thousand-dollar bond on their heads.

***

Flip heard the news in Houston and was mad and afraid. He was the one who sent Oscar and Juan to Cali to hit Nicholas. He had been told to kill Nicholas and get out of town. He chose to send two

Nicholas II A Storm is Coming

inexperienced hitters, instead of doing the job himself. Now he was going to have to clean up his mess before it came back to bite him. Flip knew the boss was going to send people to take him out because of the fuck up.

He picked up the phone and started calling friends he knew in Cali, friends he could get to help him. After three calls, he was able to reach an old friend in LA, who told him he could help.

Flip decided he was going to Cali, himself, and handle it. He felt he needed to get out of town before the boss came looking for him.

Oscar and Juan were supposed to get in around one to pick up the rest of their money. He thought about waiting for them to show and put one in each of their heads. However, he was more concerned about his own head, at the moment. He told his right-hand man to hold them, but not to kill them. He was going to fly out to Cali and clean up their mess.

***

With the morning news blasting the shooting all over the screen and radio, the streets were buzzing also. The streets knew Nicholas not only as a big-time businessman but as the Kingpin of the West Coast and an O.G. The word on the street was, Tyrone, his main man, was looking for the shooters and had a bond of five thousand on their heads.

Some thought it was a hit from the Italian Mob or Russian mob, who had been wanting to take Nicholas out for years, unsuccessfully? Some even thought, Drake Green, may have had some parts in it.

However, one thing was for sure, someone was going to talk, snitches were going to snitch; but most importantly, Tyrone was hunting and looking for answers.

***

Chapter 18

Seven hours earlier, about the time Nina's plane was climbing over the Rockies, trying to find a safe flight path, the pilot was trying to figure out why air traffic control had routed them on a northern route, when the weather was so bad over the Rockies in the first place.

While this event was occurring, a call was being placed from the San Francisco Airport to the Red Door Bar in San Francisco. After ringing several times, the bartender picked up the phone, "Red Door," he said, over the loud music from the juke box.

"May I speak to William Franklin?" a voice said, as the bartender held it to his ear. Looking around the bar, he spotted William in a booth, talking shit to some Mexican dudes.

Hold on," Cool Will," the bartender yelled, as he held the phone up in the air and pointed towards William, the two dudes sitting in the booth with him looked up along with William, as the bartender's voice boomed across the room.

William looked up while getting out the booth, going towards the bar, he picked up the phone off the bar and put it to his ear.

"This is Will, who is this?", said William, in his best pimp-in-command voice.

"This is Joey, at the airport. Are you still looking for Nicholas from Oaktown?", the bartender said into the phone, so only the person on the other end could hear.

"Yes, what do you want?", William asked, while looking back over his shoulder at the two sitting in the booth.

"Nicholas is here, and it looks like he will be here for about an hour or so."

"You telling me Nicholas is at the airport right now?"

"Yeah baby, but you have to be quick?"

Nicholas II A Storm is Coming

"I will be there in twenty minutes. Hold him there and there is three grand in it for you.

"Okay," "solid," the bartender said, and ended the call. He looked around to see if anyone was watching him.

William walked back to Oscar and Juan, and said, "Nicholas is at the airport right now, if we get out there now, we can cap him and get you guys out of town."

"We can use the old Van out back and I have the guns in my trunk. This way we don't have to go to Oaktown, that pussy has come to us!"

"Yeah, but an airport seems like a bad place to cap someone," Oscar said, while looking at Juan and William, with a lot of concern on his face.

"Oh, are you a shooter or a pussy?", William shot out.

"Watch your fucking mouth, before I put my foot in it motherfucker," replied Oscar, with a look that made William back down.

"We can catch him as he comes out the airport and be out before anyone knows what happened," said William, trying to explain the surprise.

"It just seems very risky, but I think we can do it, if we do it fast," thought Oscar, to himself.

***

Nicholas had gotten to the airport a half an hour early. However, it didn't matter, as Nina's plane was late because of bad weather across the Rockies. Deciding to have a drink, he sat at the bar across from her gate, sipping on a drink while waiting.

Nicholas had missed Nina for the past two weeks; she was back east attending her family reunion. He had wanted to go with her but had to attend a sit-down with the Mexican Cartel, along with handling some business concerning moves both him and Nina were trying to make.

The Mexican Cartel wanted Nicholas to run the West Coast operation. The drug game was really taking off, he was bigger than even he had Imagined. In a short eleven years, he had seen cocaine go from a purely social drug; to the choice of the street people, hustlers and pimps, the so-called night people. Even to the everyday person working in an office and dancing in the disco clubs, to the urban middle class in the suburbs. Cocaine based, cooked rocks, called "crack" was turning into the full-scale monster.

There was a time that you could not find an ounce of coke on the streets. Now you could find young men standing on almost every corner of the ghetto's selling rocks.

Nicholas was dead in the middle, he was the head, the reason why there is so much cocaine in the streets. Nicholas moved from selling quarter ounce bags in clubs to wholesaling to most of the western states, selling to the rich and poor alike.

Nicholas, in truth, didn't care who bought drugs, his main concern was the money. He justified his actions by telling himself that he didn't make them spend their baby's food money, or the rent money. They were grown-ass-people who had the right to do as they pleased.

Just three years ago, he helped orchestrate the police killing a dealer of his, as well as an old school friend, because the dealer started selling crack cocaine, when he told him not to. He used a classmate to pull the trigger and then allowed the police to kill the classmate in a gun fight. Nicholas felt moving crack was the wrong direction.

However, in just three years the streets were flooded with crack rocks. Everywhere you looked people wanted to suck on that glass dick. Self-greed and the incredible amount of income and financial gain proved to be too great for Nicholas to walk away from.

Now after eleven years of ducking prisons and the law, Nicholas was trying to figure a way to get out of the drug game all together. Nicholas had made his money and used it to buy and owned legitimate businesses. He didn't need the problems or the heat that drugs and crime brought.

Nicholas II A Storm is Coming

While sitting there, he started thinking about how he came up, out of the streets. How he lost his first family, behind the madness of the streets.

Nicholas thought about a saying Mr. Goldberg once told him. *"If you wanted to have something, you have to leave a little something for the next guy."*

Nicholas missed Goldberg, at times he wished he had gotten a chance to talk more with him. Goldberg was always telling him "it is not how you make money that makes you rich, it is how you use it that makes you rich." Nicholas listened to Goldberg's words, and with the help of some other people around him, Nicholas was able to build an empire.

***

Chapter 19

Blacktop, an old street hustler, and Nicholas' mentor in the drug game, was a perfect example of staying too long. The old saying, *"if you stay in this game long enough, you will either end up in prison or in the grave."*

Yes, if you stay in the game long enough, you were sure to make some mistakes. Mistakes, that in the streets, would get you killed or locked up. You only get one slip and it's over.

Blacktop's mistake was trusting, he slipped and made a sale to an undercover DEA agent, and ended up with forty years for possession with intent to sale cocaine. The government seized everything they could find, cars, houses, and most of his money. However, he still managed to stash enough to live like a king in prison.

He had set up accounts overseas and had instructed them to send monthly payments to him as retirement money. He set it up when he realized he was not going to beat the case.

Blacktop at least had a plan to live out the rest of his days. Blacktop would not likely make it out the prison system, given he was over seventy, when he started a forty-year bit. Not many black men had the knowledge or fortitude to provide for themselves.

***

Now with Juan Sanchez retiring from the Mexican Cartel, Juan left it to be run by Danny Sanchez and Jimmy Sanchez, his two sons. They wanted Nicholas to take over the whole west coast. Nicholas was faced with making an especially important decision. He was not really concerned about his people, as he saw to it, they have done very well over the years. With his guidance, they've all moved to higher levels, and for the most part were totally legitimate.

But greed and ambition can be a deterrent for common sense. With the way things were going on the streets, and with the epidemic of crack cocaine. Given the fact that crack "rock" cocaine was beginning to rear its monstrous head, Nicholas knew he had to get out. As he thought about it, he said to himself, "I'm not sure if it's greed or loyalty to Danny and Jimmy, that kept me in the game this long." But loyalty was not the motivating factor, his inner mind keeps telling him it's time to step aside. As a storm was coming, if he didn't get out now, he was going to get wet.

***

Nicholas just didn't know how he was going to tell Nina, that he was going to have to wait a year, to get out the game. He had already made moves to get all his business legitimate. He had long ago gotten all the people who helped him get started set up in their own business, showing them how to purchase stocks and bonds and use the system to make money.

To the IRS, state government, and local governments, he was strictly a successful businessman. Nicholas paid all his taxes and didn't have anyone looking for him. Sitting there, he thought about how far he had come over the past twelve years.

Nicholas no longer dealt or sold drugs directly. Everything he did was wholesale and two to three levels above the streets. To the streets, Nicholas was a ghetto legend. Nicholas was an O.G. (Original Gangster) who could have gotten out the game a long time ago.

At this moment, Nicholas was legitimate. In the eyes of city leaders, he was clean, belonging to the Chamber of Commerce, the Better Business Bureau, Black Business Chamber of Commerce, and sitting on other business boards. Nicholas had been lucky to get ahead of the game, thanks to the knowledge of older men, who taught him how to run the race.

Nicholas never wanted to be a street dealer or be known for running with a crowd. He was a loner all his life, preferring to keep his circle exceedingly small, and close. Besides Tyrone, Roland, Hazel, and Charles, very few ever approached him. Most associates were kept on a short leash. He played golf with a few associates and people but didn't do a great deal of socializing.

***

As Nicholas sat there on that stool, he thought back to the beginning. When he bought an engineering firm, and fired all the prejudiced, bigoted and racists engineers, that didn't want to work with him when he first got out of prison. He kept most of the people, but hired a number of black drafters, designers, and engineers. He then acquired a financial brokerage firm that was in receivership, and rebuilt it by funneling drug money into it, making it financially solvent. It was easy to launder a great deal of money in the unregulated stock market at the time, given the right accountant and banking people.

Hazel, one of the women who helped him get started, was a brilliant accountant. Her only set back was she was black. So, he helped her to buy a small bookkeeping company. Currently, she was the CFO of her own major accounting firm and the head accountant for Simmons Incorporated. One of the main brains behind most of his financial moves, along with Nina, who ran the company with an iron fist and calculating moves.

Hazel and Nina positioned him in real estate and encouraged him to buy homes in East, North, West Oakland and in the Hayward area. They advised Nicholas to buy an old golf course in Fremont and build a number of single-family homes. Nina helped negotiate the purchase of five high-rise properties in the downtown area, when white businesses and corporations were exiting and migrating out of Oakland.

All of this allowed Nicholas to clean a great deal of drug money. Between the engineering company and the other properties, he was able to take over a Savings and Loan association and a large mortgage company, that was in receivership, all in the past six years.

However, because of his police record and conviction, Nicholas was unable to register any businesses in his own name; therefore, Nicholas wife, Nina's name was on everything they owned. Nina held degrees in Banking, Business, and International Finance. Her knowledge helped build a multimillion-dollar business.

In 1984 alone, Simmons's Inc. paid fifty million-eight-hundred thousand in taxes to the IRS and three-million-seven-hundred thousand to the state, while making over two-hundred and three million in net profits. Nicholas, personally, has over five-hundred million in banks around the world, while maintaining over two million in several banks in and around Oaktown.

Simmons's companies have over four thousand people on various payrolls, not including crooked politicians, cops, or the people who transported drugs, or the general scumbags that live off illegal activities."

As he took a sip from his drink, he snapped out of his thoughts and back to the present. Nicholas was really looking forward to just getting away and spending time with Nina. As he heard the announcement, Nina's flight had arrived. The announcer said over the speaker's "passengers are debarking at gate twenty-six," which was across from where he was sitting. He finished his drink and placed a five on the bar, picked up the roses next to him, and walked over to the waiting area of gate twenty-six.

***

Once at home, Tyrone placed a call to the lawyer's home number, and told him what had transpired. While telling him, "get Nickels car out the San Francisco car impound and move fast", said Tyrone, with a little hint of urgency. The lawyer said that he would get right on it, and that he would have it handled within an hour.

Tyrone started calling people to find out who may have heard about the hit on Nickels. He put the word out that he wanted to know who made the move, and who was talking. Tyrone knew, *"the streets heard everything and knew before the word got to hell."* Tyrone believed it was only a matter of time before someone would start talking, and he wanted to know what the streets had to say.

It was after five in the morning when he and V climbed into bed. He hoped to get a couple of hours of sleep.

***

Tyrone got about three hours sleep before he woke up and took a shower. He then started to make calls to the others in the crew. He wanted them to be on point, and not get caught slipping. He was now going to have to step up his game. He knew those San Francisco cops were going to be all up in Nickels' business, so, his first priority was getting Nicholas moved, and then getting that car out of the impound.

He got dressed in a navy blue three-button suit and black bally shoes with a black shirt, placed his 9mm in his lower back, and started for the door. Vivian had woke up not long after him. While he was dressing, she had taken her shower and was dressed in a housecoat and a pair of flip flops. She walked up, grabbed him from behind, and said, "Going somewhere big boy, before you take care of home?", she said, with a devilish grin on her face.

"I have to go take care of some business, I was just coming to say goodbye," he said, turning around and taking her into his arms, leaning down to kiss her on the lips.

"You be careful out there and come back safe," she said. She knew trying to stop him or talk him out of going was out of the question, and that she would only be talking to the wind. So, she just let him go, and told him, "I'm going to the hospital to check on Nina, and I may go by Maria's after," she said.

"Yeah, check on her and Nick, and I will be there soon," said Tyrone. "Tell Maria hi for me also," he said, as he headed to the car. He also thought that he needed to put a couple of men around to watch over her. He was not at all sure this was finished, and he wanted to be safe.

***

Chapter 21

Tyrone met the crew in the warehouse in Emeryville. Having two things on his mind, what happened to Nicholas and Nina, and going over getting product to the distributors and dealers. He was not in a good mood. Once the crew gathered around the conference table and took seats, Tyrone began by asking Charles "how things were going on the eastside?"

"Everything seems to be good", said Charles.

"Are the boy's in the village happy with the product? I heard they were having a problem with that group from the park," Tyrone asked.

"No, they were just having a misunderstanding about who can sell where? I had a talk with that youngin name G-money, and he assures me he got a handle on it."

"Well, you keep your eye on that shit. With the FBI and DEA putting their hands in the pie, not to mention the Russians trying to get in the act, we have to keep our eyes open and ears to the ground, keep it sharp."

"I wanted to ask you about that. How do we know the Russians and not the Feds are trying to put drugs in the streets?

"We move the most product. While the product we put out can handle a six or seven hit, the shit that is getting to the streets lately is real dog shit, I hear."

"The feds are after the leaders of the Panthers, calling them dealers. Make no mistake about it, they are using undercover agents to bring weed, heroin, and coke rocks in, then bust the dealers, while telling everyone the Panthers are the reason drugs are on the streets. They put it out that the Panthers are the ones dealing and use the local pigs to bust them," said Roland, while looking around the table.

"Yeah and that fool Huey is falling right into their hands, acting like he is street smart," said Tyrone, sounding disgusted.

Nicholas II A Storm is Coming

"That is not the way the Russian's work. They just walk in and take your shit. They are not concerned about the market, they just gorilla their way," said Charles, as he added to Roland's comment.

"Well what do we do about it? We are the ones who supply the wholesale dealers, right, said John, Frances's oldest son, who took his mother's chair at the table.

That's all fine and shit, but the fact remains, make no mistake, it's the Feds who allow all drugs in the country in the first place," said Sandra, while looking at everyone.

"The boys from the city are crying the blues for better product and we are not selling anything to them," Roland stated, looking around the table like he just hit the numbers.

"Yeah, last week pops told me he was going to sit down with the Chinese and Filipinos. He was going to have a sit down and talk about the heroin market. You know they make their long money off heroin", said JR, to the rest.

"I thought we were not going to get into dealing heroin or work with the Filipinos and Chinese at all," said Roland, with a look of concern.

"Well, yes and no," stated Tyrone, while looking around the table.

***

"Look around, we are getting long in the game. It's time we start to think about getting the fuck out. This game is for the young, not the old heads we are now. Remember, when we got in this thing, the streets were different, and the people were different.

We did not go around shooting everybody for no reason, for the most parts. We did not sell on the corners and there were no rocks. We sold cocaine and people had fun. We have all made a shit pot full of money, and we own legitimate businesses. Like Nickels said, we need to move on, and get out the game, and not look back."

"I have been in this shit for over twenty years and I'm thinking about getting out while I can. I have done this thing for far too long and it is time for me to sit my old ass down. I have been training this youngster named Frank, from the lower bottom. However, I am going to talk to Nickels about it when he is better."

***

The people around the table looked at each other and each had their own thoughts but did not want to share them at the time. The thing that was at the front of their minds was how were Nicholas and Nina and what the hell happened. Before anyone could ask another question or make a statement, John, Francis son, who had taken over Vallejo, after she was confined to a wheelchair from suffering a stroke; said, what everyone wanted to ask. John was a smart young man and understood the streets. He was a part of the new blood on the streets. The streets had changed with the up rise of crack.

"With that said, how is the boss?" "Have you found out who was behind this?" asked John, while looking around the table at everyone.

With that, the table grew silent and everyone turned to Tyrone and JR for answers. JR looked at Tyrone and nodded, Tyrone looked back at JR, and begin to tell them what he knew.

"He's in a coma, but Doc says he will be okay, in time. His body must heal itself."

"Well, how long does it take for the body to heal?", asked Hazel, with a great deal of concern in her eyes.

"Doc says that it's up to Nicholas how hard he fights. The coma allows him to rest and heal," said Tyrone, and he is in good physical shape.

"What about Nina? Is she okay?", asked Sandra.

"She was hit in the neck and the shoulder, but she is doing fine. We talked to her this morning and she is getting better every minute. Doc said she may be able to get out of there tomorrow," said Tyrone.

"Now, no one outside this room knows that Nicholas or Nina are alive or where they are. We need to keep it that way, understood?", stated Tyrone, while looking at everyone at the table. They all nodded their heads, looking at each other, with the kind of acknowledgment that let you know they understood his comments.

"I will continue to look after the security and the men for them," stated Roland.

"What about Nina, will she be able to function as normal?", asked Hazel.

"Yes, she was hit, but she should recover quickly, said Tyrone.

"I got her covered, don't even worry, I have the best people on the job, and that's all day and night," said Roland, with a great deal of confidence in his voice.

Everyone was looking around and talking to themselves when Tyrone took control again.

"Hey, look, we all need to be on point. We need to get our heads on right. Remember back in 78, when we had to go to war with the Italians, we didn't panic or get scared. We handled our business and they got the fuck out our face. We don't know who is behind this, but we are going to find out. And when we do find them, we are going to handle our business," said Tyrone, loud enough for everyone to hear him.

***

They all looked at him, while they all took their seats again.

"With all the shit going on in the city, I'm going to go to the city and poke around a little. I want to see if I can find out what happened, or maybe get a handle on who is behind this," said Tyrone, as he blew a cloud of smoke across the room, and then he rubbed out his cigar in the tray.

"The news said that a van was found burned out in East Palo Alto. So, I'm going to check it out and see if I get anything, "said Tyrone, and stood up preparing to leave.

Everyone began to say their good-byes and headed toward the door. JR walked over to Devon and asked him. "Did you talk to moms this morning?"

"Yeah, I called her and told her they were in an accident, but I didn't tell her where they were. I thought I had better not let her know that info."

"Good thinking, I'm not sure she would be able to keep it to herself."

"Well, I put a couple of my boys on the block to watch her house, just in case this thing is bigger than we think," said Devon.

"That's good looking out bro," said JR, and gave him a hand slap.

After a few moments of talking to the others in the room, and saying good-bye, JR headed to his car parked next to the building.

***

Once in the car, JR's phone begins to beep. He looked at it and saw a number he didn't know. He thought about not answering, when he remembered he was waiting for Mia to call him.

"Hello, who is this?"

"Hello, yourself, is that any way to answer a phone?", said Mia, as she smiled and thought to herself, his voice sounds so sweet.

"Well, hello to you too," said JR, as he smiled and continued to head towards the freeway.

"I see you got the phone."

"Yep, a messenger delivered it about twenty minutes ago. I called you about ten minutes ago, but no answer."

"I was in a meeting and couldn't answer."

"Okay, I just wanted to let you know that I got it and thank you."

"Glad you like it, I will do anything for you, you know that."

"I hear you, but you don't have to, I can do some things for myself."

"I know, but I like doing for you. Now, I have to go handle some business, and I will talk to you later. Oh, remember to keep your phone with you at all times, if anything happens or anything comes up, call."

"Okay, but aren't these phones costly and expensive to call all the time?"

"Don't worry about the cost, its paid for by the company."

"Oh, Mr. Big Shot, huh?"

"Girl, bye."

"I love you, bye," said Mia, with a smile on her face.

"Me too," said JR, and hung up the phone.

***

H azel sat there, while everyone was talking, and wondered to herself if Nina was going to be able to make the big meeting with the bankers. As the chief accountant, she was in the know of everything they were trying to do for the family.

Nina and Hazel were scheduled to meet with the board members of the Bay Side Savings and Loan. The meeting was scheduled before Nina went back east. Now with her in the hospital, Hazel didn't know if the meeting was still on. She couldn't count on Nina or Nicholas; Tyrone was no help; he was the muscle side. She wondered who she could recruit to attend the meeting with her.

She was aware that Nicholas and Nina had shared information about the meeting with JR, so, she decided to reach out to him. JR made the most sense, as he was the oldest, and had excellent business instincts and knowledge. Like his father, he didn't act out of his feelings, he looked at all sides of the problem, before deciding on an answer. She knew he would do a good job.

Picking up her phone, she dialed JR's mobile phone. It rang three time before he answered.

"Hello, Miss Hazel", said JR, into the phone.

"Hello, JR, replied Hazel, as she thought "His mother had taught him and his brothers some manners."

"JR, I need you to sit in for Nina at a meeting on Wednesday, this week. Can you do that?"

"What kind of meeting is it? And why me? I have not been involved in any of her meetings."

"Yes, I know, but I don't want to show up by myself and want you to go with me. You don't have to talk or anything like that, just sit there and listen."

Nicholas II A Storm is Coming

"Alright, but I'm telling you I hate going around those fake-ass people."

"I hear you, can you come by my office today around three, so I can brief you on what we're trying to accomplish. Then you can look over some papers to familiarize yourself with the process, and take a minute to understand the negotiations, so far. I know that Nicholas and Nina have talked to you about the moves they are trying to make, so I will not go into that with you," said Hazel, in a very businesslike voice.

"I'll be there around three", replied JR, with some reluctance in his voice.

***

Hazel hung up her phone, walked out the warehouse, got in her car, pulling out of the warehouse parking area. She headed towards her office downtown, driving down San Pablo. As she drove, she thought back to the times she was out in the streets dealing and trying to get through school.

She had been so lucky to meet Nicholas back then. He had encouraged her to turn her life around, getting her to finish college and helped her start a small accounting business. She laundered all the money he made in the streets, along with managing the books for his engineering firm.

Now, today, she owned two buildings downtown and had several other commercial and residential properties in several states. She owned one of the biggest accounting firms on the west coast. Not bad for a poor girl from Campbell Village in Oaktown.

As she was about to pull into the underground garage of her building, she saw an old acquaintance that she knew walking across the street on Lakeside. She thought about saying hi, but changed her mind, when she thought about how they had parted company.

Not forgetting the fact that he had put his hands on her over a party she went to for one of her girlfriends in Sacramento. When Tyrone saw her face, he went off. That did not turn out good, as Tyrone broke his arm and leg and he ended up in the hospital for two weeks. *"Oh well, best let dead dogs lie,"* she thought, and continued into the parking garage.

Once in her office she told her assistant Gloria, "would you please get me Mister Anderson at the bank." "Then mark my calendar to include a meeting with Nicholas Jr. at 3:00 o'clock today? Thank you," she said, as she walked toward her office.

"Yes, I will pencil him in on your calendar. I will ring you when I have Mr. Anderson, is there anything else?", said Gloria, as she fell into step behind her and wrote on her notepad.

"No, not right now, I have some papers I need to go over, so I don't want to be disturbed; hold all calls for an hour, except the call from Mr. Anderson.

"Okay, want some coffee or a cup of tea?"

"Not now but thank you for asking. By the way, did you have a good time in Reno last weekend. You have to tell me all about it later today," said Hazel, while looking at her with a smile on her face. Her assistant stood at the door of her office with a shy embarrassed smile on her face, as she closed the door leaving her office.

She thought to herself, "yes, she did have a good weekend in Reno. She hoped that Robert, the guy she spent two days with, would grow into some type of relationship. "

Walking to her desk, she sat down and smelled the flowers he had sent her. Just the thought of last night got her wet between her legs. Snapping out of her daydream, she started to fulfill her obligations to the company, and picked up the phone to call Mr. James T Anderson, Sr, President of the Bay City Savings and Loan. When he answered the phone, she said, "hold please, for Miss Hazel Nash", in her best voice. She then pushed the button of her phone and said, Miss Nash, I have Mr. Anderson on the line. Hazel wanted to confirm the meeting and she also wanted to give him a heads up, that Nina was not going to be at the meeting.

Nicholas II A Storm is Coming

After talking to Mr. Anderson, she called Vivian to find out how Nina was doing. She was unable to reach Vivian, so she dialed JR's number and talked to him. He told her that they had not heard anything, but that Nina was doing better.

"JR, would it be okay for me to go to see her?"

"I'm not sure that is a good idea right now. We are still looking for the reason this happened".

"I know, but I need to run something by her before the meeting. I would not tell anyone where she is or bring anyone with me."

"Again, I don't think it's a good idea, but I'll run it by Uncle Tyrone; if he says it is cool then you can go but hold up until I call you."

"I'll be waiting for your call."

***

Sandra Edwards walked up to Tyrone, as everyone was leaving, and began to talk to him. "I was wondering if it would be okay, if I sent some flowers to Nina," she said, while looking at Tyrone for approval.

"I guess it would be fine as long as you're careful. We don't want to give away their location or the fact that they are alive. Can you wait until tomorrow? She should be going home, then you can send them to the house."

"I can do that. Would it be okay for me to go to the house and see her?"

"Yeah, tomorrow you can go to the house, we have people there to guard her and it's safe."

"I'll wait until she is home, it's just that we had a meeting scheduled on Thursday about a deal she was working on, and I just want to be sure we are still on track."

"I believe we are on track, but I want to be sure I have my ducks in order".

"Okay, I'll call you later today and get an update... If anything changes, please call me."

With that said, they both hugged and then headed towards their cars.

As Sandra drove back to Sacramento, she thought about the past twelve years. Sandra had obtained her degree in law and opened a firm in Sacramento where she was one of the biggest lobbyists in the state. Besides owning the law firm, she was a major player in drugs. She two had started out selling nickel and dime bags in the clubs and to assemblyman back in the day. She now ran a network of over fifty people from Sacramento to Portland.

She snapped out of her thoughts and concentrated on the road as she headed back to her office.

***

Tyrone headed to the lower bottom, he wanted to talk to his little prodigy, Frank Duke. Tyrone liked the young man, from the day he met him some twelve years ago. He liked the way he stood tall, and his hustle was strong. He had grown up in the streets, while under Tyrone's tutoring and knowledge, Frank's game had come a long way in twelve years. He supplied the lower bottom and most of Berkeley, El Cerrito, Rodeo and Hercules. Frank was gaining a reputation of his own. It would not be long before he would gain O.G. status.

As soon as he pulled up in front of the café, he noticed a couple of lookouts on both sides of the street. He spotted the two lookouts on the roof across the street, and saw they had a beam on him. Tyrone saw he was being watched from the corner of the building. He thought to himself, Frank had learned well and that he was on his game. As he walked into the café, he asked a young man walking up to him like he was a big man. "Where's Frank? Tell him Tyrone is here to see him," Tyrone boomed.

Before the words had a chance to be heard, Frank walked from out the back room and greeted Tyrone with a big smile and handshake. "Hey O.G.; what's happening?"

"I have not seen you in a while. What's happening that brings you down to the bottom?"

"Nothing great, just in the area and thought I would drop in and rap with you for a minute"

"Anytime my man, anytime, you are always welcome, you know that."

As Frank waved his hand, everybody got back to work. He walked over to a booth by the front window and sat down. He usually sat there so he could see everything coming and going on the streets.

Tyrone walked over and sat in the booth. He was about to start a conversation with Frank, but then thought better of it.

"Hey, come take a ride with me, I want to run something by you".

"Sure, I can do that"

Now Frank really felt important to be able to ride with the under boss of the city, a legendary O.G. This would really put him on the status of boss in the streets. Tyrone was not in the streets any longer, but he was still known as an O.G., and the under boss, but mostly he was still feared.

"Let's roll, I have to go to the city, and I want you to ride with me, can you handle that?"

"Can I handle that! Hell yeah, I can handle that."

"Well, we are going to the city to find someone, and when I do, I don't plan on them leaving that location, understand."

"Yeah, I understand, but the city belongs to that dude named Drake or something like that."

"Yeah, Drake Green, out of Hunters Point."

"We're going to the Point?"

"Not right this minute, we are going to look at a van first."

Once they were in the car and headed to the bridge, Tyrone turned to Frank and said, "You heard about the shooting at the airport last night?"

"Yeah, I saw that shit on the TV, at my girls house."

"That was Nickels, which was hit".

"Oh no, you are not telling me that Nickels was killed last night.

"No, I'm telling you that it was Nickels who got hit."

"He's okay then, they missed?"

"No, they didn't miss, they just didn't finish the job. I'm going to find them and finish it. I'm going to lay everyone and everything that had anything to do with it, down."

***

Chapter 23

On the other side of the bay, at an eatery, on the dock in Sausalito, three Italians sat looking out at the gate, while sipping triple expressos. Dominick Don (Baldy) Cantero, asked the others, "who gave the order, I wanna know who the fuck was it."

Anthony (The Ant) Shapero said, "I have no idea who it was, none of my people. Besides, who cares about a moolie anyway?" Looking at both while sipping his expresso. "We have a real problem here my friend, that was not just any moolie that was hit, that was Nicholas." "You all remember the last time, back in 78, when we had a conflict with Nicholas and Tyrone."

"Our wives wore black on four occasions behind that. You Dominick, lost a son and brother, and Ant you lost two son's and seventeen men, before we got them moolies to the table."

"This is not a simple problem, we need to reach out to Nicholas's people, letting them know that we did not sanction this, and we had no hand in it."

"Well, that sounds great, but I don't care about no black niggers. If I must, I'll go to war. I'm not afraid of no damn Tyrone, and yeah, he took my brother Nino out years ago.

Then the rest of the families would not allow me to touch him, but if he comes for me, on my brother's grave, I swear I will kill him," said the Ant, while waving his hands in the air and hitting the tabletop.

"Yes, my friend, we all know that you're a good man, and a fair man. But this nigger Nicholas and his partner Tyrone, should not be taken lightly, mind you, they are not like other moolies. Besides, we have too much to lose starting a war right now.

That moolie Drake Green over in Hunters Point, has everything up in arms and our police protection is running scared, because of the war he has going on in Chinatown with the Triads, as well as those Filipinos, we don't need a war with Nicholas or Tyrone."

"You're giving them too much credit, they are just two black ass niggers."

"Yeah, but Nicholas is not just a nigger. Nicholas is very smart, and he knows our ways, and don't forget he holds those books over the families that could cause a great deal of trouble for everyone, as well as the fact that he is part of the Mexican Sanchez Cartel."

"Well, like I said, I don't fear no man, Nicholas, Tyrone or whoever the fuck they are," said the Ant, while he sat back in his chair and rubbed his head.

As they talked, the telephone rang, drawing their attention. Lanza picked up the phone and answered, "hello, my friend, is he dead or what?"

"We don't know boss, there's no word on the streets. All we know is they were taken to San Francisco General and then nothing", said his top man Joe Copa.

"What the hell you mean, nothing? Find out where they are, and what happened to them. I want to know who the hitter was, you understand?"

"Yeah boss, I'm on it, I'll check back soon", said Joseph, with a look of confusion on his face.

"You find out and get back to me", said Lanza, as he hung up the phone.

"What did Joseph find out?", said Dominick.

"He's still trying to find out who did the hit. I'm going to call that Russian bastard Victor, over in Richmond, and try to determine if they know anything.

By the way, you know we have a meeting this afternoon with that Colombian," said Lanza, while standing up to look at a woman passing.

"If we are still having it at Polo's in the Tenderloin, we need to take some precautions. We need to be prepared, just in case, and put a few more men on the streets," said the Ant, while looking at each of them.

"Yes, the meeting is still on with that Colombian, but I don't trust her. From what I hear from the families in New York and Miami, she's not really a trustworthy person. Besides, I just don't like doing business with a woman," said Dominick, while looking at the Ant."

"You just mad because she won't fuck you", said the Ant, with a smile on his face.

"Fuck yourself, if I wanted to fuck her, I could fuck her anytime. I'm not like you, I don't like brown pussy," said Dominick, with a hard look at both.

A young waiter walked up, causing them to cut their conversation short. They looked out over the water toward the Golden Gate. Silently, each retreated into their own thoughts and self-fears. They all knew a storm was coming. They each had lost so much the last time a war hit the streets, both money and people. A war with Nicholas and Tyrone was a war none of them wanted.

***

Detective Moore picked up the crime report from the crime lab's box and started reading the tech's notes. The Caddy had nineteen bullet holes, mostly on the driver's side. They found fifteen 9mm bullet fragments in the car. Along the side of the road they found ten 9mm shell casings. The vans tire tracks were light truck treads, make and model, was unknown.

The lab was sending all the data to the FBI lab to see if they could ID them. The prints found on and around the car were those of Nicholas Simmons, Nina Simmons and others, including the man who helped get them out the car.

The DMV records showed the Cadillac was owned and registered to First Bay State Mortgage Investment and Holdings. An Oakland based multi-million-dollar corporation with holdings all over the western states.

Mr. Nicholas Simmons was listed as CFO of First Bay State Mortgage Investment Holding Company. He was also CEO of Simmons Engineering and several other holdings, commercial and residential properties, throughout the western states. Mrs. Nina Simmons was listed as CEO of all the companies and held a seat on the boards of several other major corporations in California.

Mrs. Simmons was a financial banker and brokerage consultant, with degrees from Penn State in Business and Finance, Howard University in Finance, and a master's from Stanford in International Finance. She was CEO of First Bay State Mortgage Investment Holding Company and her name was on other businesses as owner or co-owner.

No police records were found on Mrs. Simmons, she didn't even have a jaywalking ticket. However, the rap sheet ran red from hits on Nicholas Simmons. His rap sheet went back to the early fifties. The last thing on his sheet was his discharge from San Quentin prison in 1972, and his release from parole in 1974. He's been clean since 1972, no other arrests or incidents since his release and discharge.

 This got Detective Moore's attention. He was wondering, *"Could Nicholas Simmons be involved in a money laundering scheme?"* He wondered if the shooting was the result of crossing someone.

***

Before he could get his head around the information, his phone rang. He picked it up on the second ring.

"Hello, Moore," he said, into the phone.

"Moore, in my office", the Captain replied, and hung up.

Moore hung up the phone and looked toward the Captain's office at the other end of the room. He stood up and headed toward it. Wondering what he wanted, Moore knocked on the closed door and waited for an answer.

"Come in."

"Yeah, Captain you wanted to see me?", he said.

"Have a seat Moore," said the Captain, pointing to a chair at the table.

Nicholas II A Storm is Coming

"This is Detective Charles Booth and his partner Detective James Pardew from Oakland. They want to know what we got on that shooting at the airport last night. They seem to think it may have something to do with a kingpin over there. One they have been trying to put away for years."

Moore looked at the two detectives and acknowledged them with a nod of his head. They did the same, while the Captain went on.

"I heard on the news two people were shot. Does it have anything to do with the shootings in Chinatown or Hunters Point projects?", he asked, as he sat back in his chair.

"No, not that we know of right now, but we are working the case. We don't have much to go on yet, the people shot seem to be upright, and may have just been at the wrong place at the wrong time.

Mr. Simmons does have a past; it could be something or not. They live in Oakland, and I have been able to get general information from the data base. Thomas was going to reach out to the Oakland police, but now that they are here, maybe they can share information," said Moore, with a hint of confidence in his voice.

Booth, who sat there looking at Moore with a hint of discuss and envy, stated, "we believe Nicholas Simmons is a kingpin in drug trafficking. He has been under investigation by our department and the DEA for more than a decade."

"Well seems like you missed, we have him now and we will handle the case", said Moore.

"Let's not get in a pissing contest here," said the Captain, while leaning back in his chair, with his hands pressed on the desk.

"Well, Moore, since there are no dead bodies, what say we turn it over to Oakland, and let Booth work it. I need you working on those murders in Chinatown. The mayor wants them cleared," said the captain, with a shit-eating smile on his face, like he has said something so smart that he could not believe it himself.

"But captain I think…" Moore was cutoff in mid-sentence, "Don't think Moore, just do," Captain Doyle said, with attitude!

"I have just had city hall and the chief climbing up my ass about all the shootings in Chinatown, and all the business that has been lost, because people are not going to Chinatown, afraid of all the shootings. So, get me some answers, and a shooter, do I make myself clear?", said the Captain.

"Yes sir, I hear you, and I'll switch gears to the Chinatown case. I will give them the Simmons case." Moore walked back to his desk, throwing the Simmons case folder on the desk, and thought to himself, *"The captain had not left his desk in so long, he would not know how to get to the car."*

***

Booth and his partner left the captain's office. When they got to their car in the parking lot, Booth said to Pardew, "that asshole Moore gets on my last nerve. He thinks he is better than everyone, I wish someone would put one in his eye."

"Oh, you are just mad because he gets more than you, he is working in the city and you're not," said Pardew, with a hint of disgust in his voice.

"No, I don't care about working in the city, it's the fact that most of the cop's over here are on the take, but they act like we are secondhand stepchildren. They act like we are dirt on their shoes."

"Yeah, well most of the guys with us are just as bad, so what's your point?"

Booth didn't have an answer, he just looked at his partner and got in the car. He knew that he was taking in five hundred a week from the Italian construction company owned by the Calabro family. However, he had made his mission for the past decade to find dirt on Nicholas. Nicholas was the reason he never made Lieutenant.

He still believed Nicholas was involved, if not the orchestrator, of the shooting of two vise narcotic officers over a decade ago; however, he couldn't prove it. Given the fact that the CIA had the case sealed, and he couldn't get any information out of the department.

Now, with Nicholas being shot, he hoped that he would be able to get a foot in the door and find something on this slick-ass nigga. He hated black people and Nicholas with a passion. He would go extra hard on black men; he and his partner had the reputation of beating several men, and some believed they planted guns on a couple they shot over the past ten years.

Getting back to their office they started going over the report they got from Moore and started planning how to get Nicholas. While sitting at his desk, the phone rang, and Booth picked it up.

"Booth here," he said into the phone.

"Booth, what do you know about this thing at the airport?" said a heavy Italian accented voice.

"I have not heard anything yet, I just got the case report from the city."

"The boss wants you to get back to him and let him know if Nicholas is dead, you hear?"

"Yeah, I hear you, but I can't tell you anything I don't know, yet, give me time."

"You got two days" and the phone went dead. Booth looked around and then at the phone and thought to himself, *"if I didn't have those bills to pay, I would cut myself off from those assholes."* Then reality sat in, so he just sat there.

Finding out who was behind the shooting, and why, was going to prove to be a hard task, as the streets were not talking about a shooter. They were talking about the fact that Tyrone was on the hunt, and nobody wanted to mess around and get him on the wrong side of them.

Booth looked over at his partner, who was just hanging up his phone and said, "let's go see the wife at the hospital, she may have some information."

"Okay, shit, I just got off the phone with the SFPD impound and they have released the car. Something about a judge signed a writ this morning to release it. They didn't get to take it apart before it was gone?"

"You're telling me that they got the car that quick, and we didn't get to check it?"

"Yeah, some lawyer showed up with a signed writ, and they let him have it."

"Now I know there is something dirty going on. Let's get to the hospital before it disappears," Booth said, with a disgusting look on his face, as he headed toward the police garage.

***

Carmella walked into the restaurant dressed to the nine. The Italians where old school, beside running the docks and most of the fishing in the bay, they controlled most of the police. They were not used to dealing with a woman, but took the meeting because her reputation preceded her, and a little curiosity on their part.

The news of Nicholas being shot was not common knowledge yet. Carmella sat at the table and looked around, then she acknowledged each member of the mafia council.

Don James Lanza stated, "We are happy to meet you, but what can you do for us that we cannot do for ourselves?"

"Thank you for taking this meeting, I bring a lot to the table, and your people in New York will vouch for my credibility."

"Well, this is San Francisco not New York," said Maddie.

"I realize that, and I'm not trying to infringe or muscle, I want to set up in the Eastbay, in Oakland, and Richmond. I can make you a great offer on heroin and Colombian cocaine. My product can take a seven or eight and I have the network to move everything."

"Oh, you are just going to walk in and take over the Eastbay? You do know that we have tried for years to get rid of that nigger Nicholas. He controls that area, and so far, has been able to hold off every attempt to move him."

"I will deal with him in my own way, leave it to me. I have a plan and I will not use your people", said Carmella, as she looked at each one of them.

"We are doing pretty well on our own and have been for decades, with no problems from the Eastbay."

"Well, times are changing, and the streets are busy with young thugs and hoodlums that are killing for no reason. I want to offer a way to stop the murders and killing and get back to making money."

After an hour of talking and feeling each other out, the meeting ended with little progress. Carmella left the meeting and headed to her hotel when she thought about Nicholas.

"Did you get any word if Nicholas was dead?", she asked, her driver.

"No, I have tried everything and all I got was he was admitted to SF General Hospital and then he disappeared. No one knows where he is or if he's alive, but I'm still checking some leads," said her driver.

"I have to be sure he is dead, and we have to find those two fools who did the hit. They didn't leave as they were told. How about that William guy? Have you heard from him?"

"No, there is no word on the streets about him, no one has seen him since yesterday." Word is, he may have left town."

Okay, let's get back to the hotel, so I can figure this mess out, and get the fuck out of Cali."

***

Having driven to East Palo Alto, Frank guided the Lincoln town car along University Ave. The news report said the van was burned out in a vacant lot off University. So, that was where they were going to initiate their search. After two wrong turns they spotted the yellow tape, in a vacant lot with a burned-out van. Paying little attention to the yellow police tape, Tyrone and Frank walked onto the vacant lot, to inspect the burned-out van.

***

Looking around the lot, Tyrone noticed in the far corner a bunch of boxes and clothes partially burned. It looked as if someone was living in them. Walking off the lot Tyrone noticed an old man sitting on the other side of the street. He was just sitting with his hands up to his face and rocking back and forth.

They walked over to him, within ten feet of him they could smell the file stitch coming from his unwashed body and dirty clothes. Tyrone approached the man, "Hey there old timer, let me holler at you for a moment", he said, in a pleasant voice. "What the fuck do you wanna talk to me about?" replied the old man, not bothering to raise his head.

"Just a couple of questions my man about that van over there," answered Tyrone, getting a little upset at the wine-o for talking to him like he was some kind of fool. But he held his peace and continued to ask the wine-o questions, as he pulled a five from his pocket and handed it to the wine-o.

The old man's eyes lit up, like he saw a gift from Heaven. He took the money out of Tyrone's hand and in a quick move he was up and headed toward the gas station at the end of the block.

Tyrone and Frank kept pace with him as he made his way to the Convenience store. He went in and came out a few minutes later with a bottle of wine, sat down on a box, on the side of the store, and in one gulp, downed half the bottle. That gulp kind of stabilized and rejuvenated the old wine-o.

Over the next thirty minutes he told Tyrone and Frank about the three men who burned the van and walked away. How they went across the street to the little bar and that a white woman picked up the white boy and the two Mexicans took a cab.

By the time he finished talking, Tyrone gave him a ten, leaving him sitting on the box. They walked back to Tyrone's car and drove to the parking lot next to the little bar.

***

Tyrone and Frank entered the First Pole bar. A dimly lit single room with a race track décor, with lots of race track memorabilia, a marble bar top along the right side, and a few stools decorated with saddle like seats, a couple of tables with a juke box on the left wall, and a small bandstand crammed in the left corner in the rear. They took stools at the bar.

The bartender was a short white man with brown hair, wearing a jockey cap and jersey, he walked up, placing a napkin on the bar, and asked, "What will it be gent's?"

"I'll have Johnny Red," said Tyrone, while looking around the little bar.

"Make mine a shot of JB," said Frank, as he looked at the pictures of horses on the wall.

"Hey bartender, were you working last night?", inquired Tyrone, as he took a sip of his drink in a serious tone of voice.

"No, I wasn't working last night...Sam the owner was... Why you asking... I started my shift eleven this morning. The boss, Sam, may be in about four or so," he replied, and walked to the register to get change for the fifty Tyrone laid on the bar.

Tyrone looked at his watch, seeing that it was almost four, he told Frank they were going to wait for the owner. Sitting at the bar sipping their drinks, Tyrone thought about the information the wine-o gave him, while trying to piece together the events of last night.

A B Hudson

While he was thinking, the owner, Sam Ellis, walked in with a bank deposit bag and headed to the register behind the bar.

***

Sam placed the bag under the bar, as he continued to count the money in the register. The bartender called out to him while washing a dirty glass at the other end of the bar. "Hey Sam... these gentlemen are waiting to talk to you."

Sam turned at the call of his name and looked at the two black men at the bar. He didn't recognize either one, so he was a little suspicious, he's cautious as he approached them. Sam walked up to the two men and stood with his hands on the bar as he leaned on the bar, "how can I help you gents?", said the Irish Italian with his Italian accent.

"I would like to talk to you about what you might have seen last night," stated Tyrone, with a little hint of bass in his voice.

"What do you mean talk... I was busy most of the night, the fights were on and we did rather good", replied Sam, with a hint of pride in his voice.

"I need to know if you saw a white man with two Mexicans come in last night," stated Tyrone, not wanting to waste time, so he got right to the point.

"Like I said there was a lot going on... One of my girls didn't show, so I had to work the bar alone", said Sam, looking at Tyrone, and thinking, like who is this fool? I don't have to talk to him.

"They would have come in sometime after seven...After the fire around the corner", stated Tyrone, while looking at Sam for any signs of lying.

Frank sat there and watched the rest of the people in the bar and kept an eye on the other bartender.

Tyrone pulled a fifty from his pocket and laid it on the bar.

"Well, I do seem to remember a funny talking white guy with a couple of wetbacks ... They walked in about that time," said Sam, trying to remember the three.

"Did you get a good look at them... What did they look like? It's important that I find them... as I told you?", replied Tyrone, while placing another fifty-dollar bill on the bar.

Sam looked at the money and thought a little harder. It's funny how money can get your mind to remember.

"I can tell you the white guy was some type of clown, by the way he talked, and the clown ass clothes he had on... He sounded like a brother when he talked, but only you could tell he wasn't a real brother, if you know what I mean," stated Sam, while reaching behind him and getting a bottle. He poured himself a shot of Irish whiskey while refreshing Tyrone and Frank's drinks.

"How long did they stay...was there anyone else with them?", asked Tyrone, in a calm voice.

"No, they were here alone...I guess about an hour or so, until a white woman came in to meet up with them," replied Sam.

"What did she look like?", asked Tyrone.

"She was a looker...you could see she was high maintenance ... I would say she was with the white guy...she gave him a big kiss and sat next to him."

"What happened next?"

"After a few minutes, they all got up, paid with a hundred and left a twenty", Sam said, smiling.

Anything else you can tell me?" said Tyrone.

"I watched them on the monitor in the parking lot. The white guy and the woman got in a new grey Mercedes," said Sam, with a hint of envy in his voice.

A B Hudson

"What about the two Mexicans?", asked Tyrone, trying to get a picture in his mind of the two. "They didn't get In the Mercedes?", asked Tyrone, with a strange look.

"They stood next to the car and the white guy handed them a briefcase and then they walked across the street to the gas station... I didn't pay them anymore attention after that," said Sam, while taking the two fifty's and putting them in his pocket. Tyrone and Frank sat there and finished their drink. "I want to know who this white guy is and who is the woman," said Tyrone.

"Well boss, we know that he drives a Mercedes," said Frank.

"Hey, wait a minute, he said, he looked at the monitor," replied Frank. "He must have it on tape, right?"

"Good looking out," said Tyrone, as he called Sam over.

"Hey Sam, I want to look at the tape from the parking lot?", Tyrone asked.

"Come to my office in the back," said Sam, as he led the way. The tape was not that great, but they could make out the license plate and get a decent look at the four people on the video tape. It was after six when Tyrone and Frank headed back to Oaktown with the information they had gotten from the wine-o and Sam. Tyrone told Frank that he would pick him up around ten in the morning and left.

***

Chapter 25

Vivian sat in the kitchen wondering who would want to shoot Nicholas, he was no longer dealing in the streets. He was far removed from the day to day business and only handled the wholesale. Finishing her coffee and cleaning up the kitchen, she went up to her bedroom. She went to her walk-in closet, took out a nice little blue dress, one she had bought in New York on a shopping trip with Nina. She decided on a pair of blue Italian heels.

After dressing, she decided to drive the BMW, she thought she might stop at a little shop on Market and see if they had gotten anything new. Grabbing her red fox coat and keys, she headed to the hospital.

She was annoyed when she saw the sign at the entrance saying, full; she drove around the hospital a couple of times, before she was able to find a parking spot, and it was a full block down the hill from the hospital.

She was walking in heels and cussing everybody parked in the parking lot. When she finally got to the hospital's main door, she was even angrier to find out they had valet parking and that they would have taken her car and parked it. The only thing that prevented her from going the fuck off on the valet was Maria pulled up in her little red mustang GT, stepped out, handing the valet her keys.

"Hey, are you just getting here?", Maria asked, with a smile.

"No, I just walked up that damn hill, I parked a block away and had to walk," Vivian said, still angry from walking in six-inch heels.

"Yeah girl, I did that once. I didn't know about valet parking and walked two blocks in heels to see my mother last year", said Maria, in a calm voice.

***

When detectives Booth and Pardew got to the hospital, they asked to speak to Dr. Becker. The duty nurse informed them that Dr. Becker was not on duty. She informed them that he may be in the Doctor's lounge sleep, or he may have left the hospital.

"Would you please check and get him for us?", Detective Booth said, with a voice of authority. The duty nurse went to the Doctor's lounge. Dr. Becker was sitting at a little desk writing instructions for other patients.

"Dr. Becker, excuse me," the nurse said, as she entered the room.

"Yes," he said, as he looked up from the desk.

"There are two detectives out front that want to talk to you", she said, looking at him with concern on her face.

"Okay, I will be there in a moment", he replied, while continuing to write his instructions.

When he arrived at the emergency room, about ten minutes had gone by.

"Detective Booth," Dr. Becker said, as he held his hand out to shake hands.

"Good Morning Doctor, we would like to ask you a couple of questions about your patient, Nina Simmons," Booth said, and looked at the Doctor with a little suspicion.

"Not a problem detectives, let's go into the coffee area to talk."

Going into the coffee area, Dr. Becker went right to the coffee table, and poured himself a cup of coffee and then turned and asked, "Would you like a cup?"

"No thanks, I've had my cup for today", said Pardew.

Booth looked at the doctor and said in a calm voice,

"What can you tell us about Mrs. Simmons?", taking out his notepad to write his reply.

"Where did they hit her Doc?", asked Booth, writing in a small notebook, as his partner looked on.

"Let me take a look at the chart. It appears she had three wounds, the one to her neck was the most dangerous. It had missed her vital organs by mere centimeters. Had it hit the jugular vein she would have bled out in minutes," he said, as he took a sip of his coffee.

"She also had a hole in her left hand, which I believe was caused by the bullet in her left arm, which I was able to remove," Dr. Becker stated.

Detective Booth listened to the doctor and thought to himself *"I still cannot figure this shooting."*

"Dr. Becker, would you have all the bullets you removed sent to the police lab in Oakland right away please?", Booth said.

"Alright detectives, I will have them sent to the lab, and yes, you can speak to her; I believe she is on the fifth floor," the doctor stated.

"Thank you, Doctor, we will be talking to you," Detective Booth said, still deep in thought, as he and his partner headed to the elevator.

***

Booth and his partner got off the elevator on the fifth floor. He hopes to get a statement that would help him find out what happened. They walked to the nurse's station and asked to speak to Mrs. Nina Simmons. The nurse at the station directed them to room 534.

When they got to the room, they were told by a young nurse that they would have to come back in a couple of hours, as her doctor was running some test on Mrs. Simmons, they could not see her right then.

Booth then asked to speak to the doctor. He was told Doctor Logan would be available in a couple of hours. So, Booth and his partner walked back to their car.

***

Booth and his partner returned to the hospital about three in the afternoon. He found Mrs. Simmons awoke. He walked into the room to find Maria sitting in the chair next to the bed and Nina sitting up in the bed. Nina was in a little better condition than she was earlier. Maria had combed her hair, cleaned her up and applied a little makeup. Nina still did not feel great, but she was a lot better, and the meds were working.

"Good afternoon, Mrs. Simmons, my name is detective Booth, and this is detective Pardew, we're with the Oakland Police Department," he said, holding his badge up for her to see.

"Good Afternoon, what can I do for you?", Nina replied, looking at the badge and then at them. Nina had no expression or concern in her voice.

"I realize you are still under care and that you may not feel like talking, but we have to ask you a few questions about last night," Booth said, trying to sound courteous.

"Well officers, I don't remember much about the accident. I woke up here in the hospital, so I don't know how much help I can be," Nina replied.

"Well, the first question I need to ask, is did you see who shot at you?

"No, like I said I don't remember the accident, other than my husband yelling to duck," she said, with a little sour note in her voice.

"Well, can you tell me what you were doing just before the accident?"

"We were leaving the parking garage heading to dinner in the city. I had just placed the roses he brought me on the floor, when he yelled, duck! From that point on, I don't remember much. Oh yes, I do seem to recall someone pulling me out of the car and then everything went black and I woke up here in this bed," she said, and looked directly at him.

"Well, Mrs. Simmons I'm sorry for all the questions, but that's how we are going to find the ones who did this," he said, while looking directly at her.

"One other thing, do you know of anyone that may have wanted to shoot your husband or yourself?"

"No, I don't know of any reason someone would want to shoot at us," Nina replied.

"If you think of anything else would you please call my office?" , he said, and handed her his card.

***

Detective Booth and Pardew walked back to their car in the police parking lot, talking about the answers Mrs. Simmons gave them.

"I still don't get the reason for the shooting," Booth said.

"Yeah, she seems to be holding something back," Pardew said.

"Seems like she knows a lot more than she's willing to tell, but what?" Booth replied.

"Look at it like this, if it was a hit, who would want it, and what are they into?" Pardew replied.

"Yeah, but she doesn't fit the profile for it to be a hit," Booth said, as they reached their car and got in.

***

P-Slim wanted the rest of his money for the information he and Dirty Mike had given to William. Having watched the news about the shooting at the airport, he was in a panic. William owed him five grand, the other half of the ten thousand promised.

He picked up the phone and called the Red Door Bar. He asked to talk to William Franklin, the bartender said he had not seen William, but he would tell him when he saw him. P-Slim hung up the phone and wondered if William had been killed. He didn't know where William laid his head, but knew he lived somewhere in Berkeley. Finding him was the most important thing he had to do, his life depended on it.

Just as he was about to leave, the phone rang, and he answered it. "P, have you heard Nicholas is not dead", said Dirty Mike, sounding full of fear.

"Yeah, be cool and get a hold of yourself", replied, P-Slim trying to sound confident.

"We don't have anything to fear, no one knows we were the ones who fingered Nicholas", replied, P-Slim, sounding somewhat fearful.

"Yeah, I hear all of that, but I don't want Tyrone coming after me. So, I'm getting my black ass out of town. You can do what you want, but I'm out", said Dirty Mike.

"Wait... wait don't... don't do anything... not until we get the rest of the money" said P-Slim.

"How we going to get something when we can't find William. That nigger could be dead already, for all we know, no, I'm out. I don't care about the money; I just want to keep on breathing. I'm going to Bakersfield... I can stay with a girl I know down there. I'll talk to you later", said Dirty Mike, and hung up the phone.

P-Slim stood there for a moment and thought he had better get in the wind also, but he didn't have a clue where he could go. He didn't have but about two thousand in cash and that would not get him far. He decided he was going to try to find William and get the rest of the money William owed him.

He got in his car and started to drive towards Berkeley, hoping he would find someone who knew where to find William. He knew it was a long shot, but he didn't have a lot of choices. If he didn't find William by the afternoon, he was going to head to Reno.

***

William and Susan had driven from East Palo Alto to his home in the Kingsland district in the Berkeley Hills. He and Susan were going to get out of the country. But he first had to get a passport, and some money moved. William knew that he was not a killer and that he couldn't go to jail, but his greatest fear was Carmella or someone coming to get him.

William looked at his pager and saw 6969 and knew that it was P-Slim paging him. He knew that P-Slim wanted the rest of the ten thousand he promised him for the information. But William was not leaving the house after he heard on the morning news that Nicholas was not dead. He was now even more paranoid and afraid then he was last night.

William called P-Slim, "Hello, you paged me?"

"Yeah, said P-Slim... I need to get at you about my money... meet me here at the pier and get this done?", stated P-Slim, with a strong voice.

"Oh, hey my man, let me get at you tomorrow", said William, trying to sound calm.

"Oh, hell no...I want my bread now right now," said P-Slim, thinking William was trying to slip him a fast one.

"Hold up my man, I'm busy right now, I have to get at you later," replied William.

"No, I want my bread and I want it now, I'm at the bait shop at the pier; you better be here with my bread in an hour or I'll be coming for you...understand what I'm saying?", said P-Slim, with a lot of attitude.

"Okay…Okay, I'll be there, I have something I need to handle", replied William, looking at the money on the table.

"Bring me my money, I'm waiting", said P-Slim, and hung up the phone.

***

Chapter 27

Nina was getting ready to leave the hospital after being there for two days. Doctor Logan felt she could continue to heal at home. She was still wearing the brace, it aided in holding her head still, so the wound would be able to heal correctly.

Vivian and Maria had come to take her home. Nina sat in the wheelchair, as Maria rolled her to the administration office to sign her discharge papers. Nicholas had been moved to Alameda Hospital. Nina knew that Nicholas had enemies in the city, and she wanted him safe. The fact that they did not know yet who was behind the shooting or if they would try again, she wanted to be smart, and get him where she could be sure he would not be in harm's way.

***

When she got to the house, she was tired and sore from the drive and wanted to rest. Vivian and Maria stayed there to help her. Vivian had hired a maid, a nurse, and a cook to help. Roland had sent four security guards to watch her. They were there to watch for anyone coming to the house, watch for any suspicious cars or trucks driving around the area, to stop anyone who came to the door for any reason; they were there to make sure nobody got into the house.

***

The first night home Nina was unable to get any sleep. When she did fall off to sleep, she dreamed about hitting the pole. The next morning, she was a mess and wanted to get a good hot bath, but the brace was not going to allow her to get in a tub. The nurse that Vivian had hired was there to help her get washed up and handle her daily hygiene. It felt good to have her body washed. The nurse combed her hair and removed the bed pan. Nina felt embarrassed having someone clean her like she was a baby; however, she couldn't do it for herself and so she was somewhat appreciative for the care the nurse took with her.

She was dressed in a tan silk gown with yellow roses. The nurse checked the IV in her arm and made sure the meds were flowing correctly. She was going by the instructions Doctor Logan wrote In Nina's chart. She asked, "Mrs. Simmons, is there anything else you need or want."

"No, I think I can rest now", replied Nina.

Nina thought about the fact that Nicholas had been moved to Alameda Hospital. She decided she was going to get dressed and go see him. Calling for the nurse, she told her to get a light pink dress out of her closet and a pair of low heels. She didn't realize she didn't have any flats that she could wear. She had worn high heels for so long, she didn't remember the last time she had purchased a pair of flats.

***

With Doctor Logan overseeing Nicholas move from San Francisco General Hospital to Alameda Hospital, Nina informed the two security guards that they were not to allow anyone other than his doctor, and the assigned nurse, to see, or move Nicholas, without calling her.

Nina was hungry but did not want to eat. She needed to find out if the move of Nickels went well and how he was doing. She called Alameda hospital and asked for Doctor Logan, Nick's doctor. He told her everything went well, and they had moved Nickels okay.

Doctor Logan told her that there was no change in his condition. Nickels was still in a chemically induced coma and resting. He assured her Nicholas was not in pain or having any discomfort. Dr. Logan said he called a private nursing agency that he used all the time. He told Nina he had hired three nurses from the agency. One nurse from 6am to 3pm. One from 3pm to 12 midnight, one from midnight to 6 am.

"I have used the agency before and they are the best nurse staffing agency in the state."

"I will be checking on him and will be on call."

"Fine doctor, don't cut on the cost, get the best," Nina said, and hung up the phone.

She then called Tyrone and told him what the doctor had said.

"I know his doctor is good and has a good heart, but I want to be sure that no one gets to Nick in that hospital."

"I hear you baby girl, I have men on the floor with him and outside 24/7, no one is getting in there, without us knowing".

"How is the search going, have you heard anything?"

"Yes, I have some leads I'm working on, more will be coming. It's only a matter of time before the streets will start to talk, you can bank that shit."

"I know you are on the case; I love you for that but be careful yourself. If they came at him, they may be dumb enough to come at you."

"I wish they would. I have not had any fun in a minute."

"Enough talking about me, how are you feeling baby girl?"

"I'm doing fine, V and Maria will not let me pee without trying to help me."

"You don't realize how much V loves you. She doesn't have any family here and to her, you are family"

"Well, let me get off this phone and take care of some other business that can't wait."

***

Nina sat up in the bed, and told Maria that she wanted something to eat, and to dial a number for her. Maria called down to the housekeeper and asked her to bring the food, she then picked up the phone and dialed the number Nina had handed to her and handed the phone to Nina.

"Hello, who is this?"

"Hello, this is Nina, is this Danny?"

"Who is this again?"

"This is Nina Simmons, Nickels wife. "

"Well, I have not heard from you in a while. How is my friend Nick doing?"

"He was shot three nights ago at the airport."

"He was what!", Danny said, in a loud voice.

"Who in hell shot him?", Danny asked, with a great deal of anger in his voice.

"We don't have all the answers yet. I just wanted to touch base with you and let you know everything is cool," Nina stated, trying to remain calm.

"Is he gone?", Danny said, with a lot of concern and sympathy in his voice.

"No! Nina shot back; he is not gone. I moved him to a safe place and have placed security around him," Nina replied.

"That's good, I can have Carlos and a couple of my men come up there and help you, if you want."

"No, I can handle it, but thanks. I will call you just as soon as I have any more news. We can handle everything as usual, on time as always; I will talk to you later," Nina replied, speaking in code. She hung up the phone just as the housekeeper walked in with a tray full of food for her and Maria.

She sat up in bed and ate the baked chicken and brown rice, the cook had prepared for her, it was delicious, Maria ate with her. The cook had prepared her favorite dessert, crusted apple pie with a scoop of vanilla ice cream on top.

***

"Girl, I have to go, I just talked to Vivian and she will be here in a minute. I have to get home and change, I got a date with that tall piece of chocolate, Roland, with his fine ass," said Maria, while wiping her mouth, and placing the napkin back on her tray.

"Maria, you dog, I know you are not messing around with Nick's boy, Roland," Nina said, rolling her eyes at her.

"Just a little something I wanted to try," Maria replied, holding her index finger and thumb up, to show just a little space between them with a smile.

"It is not like I'm going to marry the dude, I just want a little of that pipe I see he's got", Maria said, with a great deal of lust in her voice, while stretching her hands wide.

"Girl, you better not hurt him," Nina said, and laughed.

"He's a big boy, and I'm sure he will be more than happy when he hits this," Maria said, as she patted her fat ass with her right hand.

Vivian walked in the room as the two of them were laughing like two schoolgirls on a sleep over.

"What's so funny? You are acting like two ho's, at a pimp convention.

"Hey, hi to you, and fuck you too", Maria said, and hugged Vivian while smiling back at Nina lying on the bed, still laughing.

"We were just having a little girl talk", replied Nina, through her laughing fit.

"Yeah, nothing that you would care about," added Maria, trying to calm down.

"Well then, share the news, and let me be the judge," Vivian said, and looked at Maria with a little smile across her lips and her hand on her chest. Nina let the cat out the bag.

"She has a date with one of Nick's boys," blurted out Nina, before Maria could answer.

"She what? You are telling me you are dating one of Nick's boy's, which one?", Vivian asked, looking at Maria who was getting up to put on her coat. Maria looked back from the door and said, "You don't need to know, I will let you know if I like him after tonight, now get out my business and get some of your own ho's', I'm out."

With that statement, Maria left them both with their mouths opened and silly grins on their faces. She didn't want to go into all the details about Roland and her. She thought to herself "*I should not have told Nina about Roland until I had found out if it was cool. Oh well, fuck it, I have done it, so fuck it.*" She snapped out of her thoughts and drove home to change.

***

Chapter 28

The same day Nina went home from the hospital, Tyrone had gotten the information on who owned the grey Mercedes he saw on Sam's tape. Turned out that the car belonged to William Franklin, the son of Carl Franklin, an old friend of Nicholas and his first major connection. Carl had been dead for five years and his son William was a fuck up and wannabe player. He hung around brothers and tried to act like a brother but could not pull it off. He got ho's to talk to him and even one or two to work, but he was a trick and would end up losing them. Just a rich boy wanting to be a pimp.

***

The two Mexican's were a different story. The word on the streets was they were not from here. Some thought they were from Mexico, while others placed them down south in Texas or maybe even Cuba. Tyrone knew they had gone to the San Jose Airport by cab the night of the shooting. However, by the time they got there the last flight had gone and the airport was locked down for the night. So, he knew they had to stay in San Jose for the night and catch a flight in the morning.

Tyrone and Frank, two days after the shooting, went to the airport and asked around. They first looked it the schedule of flights on the big board. There were four flights that left early. The first flight was to New York, the second was to Chicago, the third one was to Denver and the fourth to LA.

They checked at the ticket counters for each, asking the agents if they remembered two Mexican's buying a one-way ticket. They found that two Mexican men did walk up and buy a one-way ticket. They bought a ticket to Denver with connections to Houston, and paid cash for the ticket. The agent said they didn't have any baggage to check.

Tyrone was mad that they had got away from him for the moment, but he knew he was going to track them down. It was just a matter of time. They would make a mistake and he was going to be there.

***

Nickels remained in a coma. There was no word on the whereabouts of William. Tyrone got a call from a guy who claimed he knew who shot Nicholas, but it turned out the guy was just talking shit. It cost him his life, as Tyrone put a bullet in his head for wasting his time and trying to con him.

That action got the attention of the streets. Word got out that Tyrone was in monster mode. Everyone knew that a storm was coming, dark clouds and thunder and lightning. The thunder was the noise on the streets and the lightning the flash of the gun.

With Thanksgiving only three weeks away, the streets were full of junkies and crack heads, trying to get in where they could and to get their dope. The stores were watching for the booster's, and for the robbers.

But given the money Tyrone had put on William's head it was a sure bet that someone was going to talk. Tyrone drove to the pool hall on 73rd and MacArthur Blvd. He owned it but had a couple old school hustlers manage it. The pool room had a notorious reputation. Everything and anything that was going on in the streets, would get to the pool hall. It was like a library of information. Tyrone knew if it happened, on the streets of Oaktown or in the bay; it was a lead pipe cinch to be talked about in the pool halls, barber shops and local corner bars.

That was the biggest weakness of the streets, anything that happened in the dark was sure to come to the light. Someone was going to brag or talk about it or knew the one who did it. It never failed, the grapevine on the street had information before the devil even knew it happened.

***

James, aka the mouth, managed Tyrone's pool hall, an old school hustler who had gotten out the game a few years back. James used to run one of the largest dice games in the city, but that ended when some young fools shot up the place killing three cops in the process. Since then, James worked and managed the pool hall for Tyrone. James continued to run a nice little dice game on the side but kept it on the low. A great deal of information came through the doors by way of the streets talking and fools running their mouths.

Tyrone played a few games of eight ball, hanging for a couple of hours, looked over the books and thought about the information that he had gotten from East Palo Alto.

However, he still didn't have a name for the one who ordered the hit. He now knew the two Mexicans were in the wind. He knew they came from Houston, but he still needed their names. Houston had a couple of Kingpins and was open turf.

Nicholas did not supply the state and didn't visit it. Texas belonged to the El Paso Cartel run by Carlos the son of one of the founders of the Mexican Cartel. Carlos and Nicholas were nowhere near friends on any level. Texas was an open state, some of the families from the east coast had people there and they had an understanding going that anyone could deal.

Tyrone heard that a Colombian group had started to move their operation into Houston and Dallas a couple of months ago. Not knowing who ordered the hit was a big problem for him, because he needed to make sure they never tried this again. Even with Nicholas getting out the game, He could not let anyone get away with this kind of disrespect. Tyrone sat there and thought about all the people who may have had a problem with Nickels and himself.

Tyrone thought about Drake Green out of Hunter's Point. He knew Drake and Nickels had history that went back. Nevertheless, Drake was not foolish enough to order a hit. He was in the middle of a war with the Filipinos and Chinese. Besides, he was moving towards heroin and not cocaine anyway. However, Tyrone was going to check him out just to be sure.

***

"The Name of the Game" was a local club on the north side of town known for having eyes and ears on the streets. It's the main watering hole for some of the biggest, boldest pimps, hustlers, and notorious drug dealers and O.G.'s in Oaktown. The Game was the place to be if you wanted to be a player. Tyrone pulled into the parking lot, found a spot, and cut the engine.

He knew that if anything was happening in the world of pimps, street dealers, hustlers, and players; somehow it made its way to the Game. He walked in and took a seat at the bar. The bartender, an old street hustler walked up, placed a napkin on the bar top. "Well, what's happening O.G.? Haven't seen you in a while, how's it hanging?" said Jerry, reaching over the bar and slapping Tyrone's hand.

"It's hanging my man, I 'm on my job, I just stopped to see what the word was on the streets," said Tyrone, as he looked around the bar.

"Man, I was thinking about Nick last night. I played golf with Nick Saturday morning, he was in a good mood, as his lady was coming home. Go's to show, you never know when the game is going to bite you", replied Jerry, as he poured Tyrone a glass of Johnny Walker Black label.

"Yeah, it's a cold world out here. One never knows when he is going to have to hold court or not", said Tyrone, while taking a sip of his drink.

"Well, what can I do for you? You know me and Nick go back... anything I can do just ask", said Jerry, with a bit of sorrow in his voice.

"I'm looking for a dude name William Franklin, I need to talk to him", said Tyrone, with a little hint of anger in his voice.

"Don't know the dude, but I have heard, he hangs with a couple of wannabes named P-Slim and Dirty Mike. Those two are dirt and for my money they would snitch in a minute. They don't hang around here. I'm told they hang at a club in the city called the Red Door. I hope you get the sons of bitches that hit Nick", said Jerry, with an honest look of regret on his face.

Tyrone sat there and talked to Jerry while he finished his drink and placed a twenty on the bar and left.

***

Chapter 29

The thing about the streets is everyone wants fame, and they want others to know they are the shit. The biggest and boldest hustlers and players were out there telling on themselves, with all the bragging, and shit talking; about how they did this and how they did that. One need only wait, and someone would tell it.

I planned to sit in the cut and watch. So far, there had been no information or any word on the airport. However, I knew it was only a matter of time. I was offering a grand for information and for that kind of money; a mother would turn on her child.

***

The day after, Tyrone and Frank, went to a couple of local bars in North Oakland, they got word that William was trying to buy some papers. Word was he was hiding in a motel outside of Vallejo by Dixon.

That clue pointed to a guy whose reputation as a forger was only surpassed by his reputation as an alcoholic. Carl Mann was a check writer and forger. For the right price, you could get a new license, social security card, passport or even a birth certificate, if your money was right.

Carl Mann worked out of a neighborhood bar called Johnny 77, so Tyrone and Frank were headed there to get a handle on Carl's location. When they got to the bar, they found out that Carl had not been in for a couple of days. The bartender said he could be working or in jail, he was not sure. But he did say Carl had a girl who lived in Richmond. Somewhere around 47th near the city center. Frank gave the bartender a twenty and told him if he saw Carl, to call him, and gave him a card.

"By the way, by any chance have you seen a dude that goes by the name P-Slim", asked Tyrone, out of the blue, as they finished their beer.

"You mean Dirty-Mike's homeboy?", replied the bartender, with a suspicious look on his face.

"Yeah, that's the one, I want to talk to him, have you seen him or not", replied Tyrone.

"Yeah, he was in here a couple of days ago looking for that white boy who calls himself (Silk William) or something. A wannabe, but a ho's dream if you know what I mean", replied the bartender.

"Do you know where we can put our hands on him", asked Frank?

"No, he doesn't hang out here, but he does eat now and then at that diner across the street."

***

William needed to get a hold of Carl, to get his and Susan's new names and papers. He called Johnny 77 and talked to the bartender, "Have you seen Carl around?"

"No, he hasn't been around for a couple of days, he may be locked up again."

"Well, if you see him, tell him to hit William up, I have some business for him."

"Okay, I will pass it on", replied the bartender, and hung up.

Carl heard that William was looking for him, and knew it had to do with getting or wanting some new documents. He could make a few thousand quick. He got in touch with William through a friend and told William to meet him at Johnny 77 on San Pablo in an Hour.

William drove to the club and met with Carl. He told him he wanted new passports, licenses, birth certificates and social security cards, with new names, for both him and Susan and he wanted them fast.

Carl listened to Williams talk and thought to himself, "*I can make ten thousand on this one.* "

"Okay, I can do all of that, but it's gonna cost you ten thousand for the package. Half now, and the other half when I deliver the documents", stated Carl, in a business voice.

"Okay, but how long will that be? I need the package right away", said William.

"Give me three days and I will have them."

"Okay...I will bring you the money tonight."

"I will start when I get the money and bring a number that I can reach you at when I'm ready."

With the business done, William got up and left. He didn't like being in the streets when people were looking for him. He was going to go get Susan and head out of town or at best get a motel somewhere he was not known.

***

Chapter 30

Tyrone knew that Nickels was planning to get out the game, because he and Nina wanted to start a family. Vivian had brought up getting married a couple of times. He gave in to her and asked her to marry him. She was so happy when he gave her an engagement ring, and she called everybody to tell them she was getting married, and how big the diamonds were in her ring.

Like Nick, he was getting long in the game and time was running out. The streets are not the place where one could grow old, every day was a new kind of hell out there.

The young thugs wanted what you had and were hungry enough to come for you, if they thought you were weak. The rules of the streets were the strongest survived and the weak died, this was the word everyone lived by day in and day out.

Tyrone thought about Danny and Jimmy, the west coast bosses of the Cartel. Could they have placed a hit on Nickels because he wanted to get out? He dismissed that thought as Danny and Jimmy went back to diapers with Nicholas.

The Cartel was big and if Nickels left the game, it would leave a big hole. However, Nickels had told them that if he were to retire, he would raise a new kingpin to take his place, and business would go on as usual. Growing tired of the shit the youngster's playing pool were talking, Tyrone decided to head out.

***

Oscar and Juan were at the Denver airport changing planes, when Oscar called his woman in Houston. He told her to pick him up at the airport. She told him that two men had been by the apartment looking for him. She also told him the word on the street was, Flip had placed a bond, on Juan and him.

"What the fuck are you talking about?" asked Oscar, trying to understand what she was saying.

Nicholas II A Storm is Coming

"Two men came by about an hour ago and they wanted to know where you were. I told them I had not seen you for three days...they hit me a couple of times, but I got them to leave me alone", said Jackie, in a low voice with no shame.

"You did what...listen to me, go to the back of the closet and get that shoebox. Then I want you to pack our clothes...everything you can get in two bags... When you are done, drive out to the Texas Steakhouse. You know the one by the airport and wait. I'll meet you there, understand?"

"Yes, I understand, but why there...Why don't I just pick you up at the airport when you land? What is happening Oscar, I don't want to get in any trouble with Flip."

"Just do what I say, and don't talk to anyone. Jackie, please check that you are not followed."

"Okay, what time will you be there?"

"I will be there when I get there, you just wait in the car, I will find you."

"What time is your plane getting in?

"We'll be landing about one. That's two hours from now. I have to go now, see you in a couple of hours."

With that, Oscar hung up the phone and headed to the gate for his plane. Juan was already sitting there waiting to board.

"How is everything in Houston, is Jackie happy you are coming home?"

"Yes, she is...and everything is up in the air...she told me two guys came by looking for me."

"Flight 254 for Houston is ready to board. Please have your boarding pass ready and present it to board. First class may board at this time. Thank you", said the attendant over the mike.

"Oscar and Juan got up and boarded the plane. Both of them sat in first class and thought about their own problems and dreams.

Oscar and Jackie drove from Houston to Dallas. Oscar wanted to get away from Houston until he could figure out what had happened to turn Flip on him.

Flip and Roberto had both placed a bond on his head. He knew he had fucked up and was going to have to lay low for a moment.

Now, three days after the shooting, Oscar and Jackie were in the Doubletree Hotel in San Jose. Jackie was turning tricks out of the hundred Grand Club and walking the streets. Oscar was laying low while he looked for a connection to buy some cocaine.

He had just over seventy-five thousand to get started with his plan. He thought about getting a good connection and how much he could get for fifty grand. He only came out to eat and try to get an understanding of who the players were who ran the streets.

Jackie was an exceptionally good ho; she knew how to make money. Besides, she loved to fuck. She would work from early evening until the clubs closed in the morning. She also knew how to cook crack cocaine.

***

Luke Carrillo was the big dog on the block, the main supplier of drugs in the San Jose area. He had a deal going with some biker's out of a small town in the valley named Merced. They provided him with weed and coke. At the time he was getting his heroin from his cuz in Los Angeles. Luke moved about ten kilo's a week, with five houses located around San Jose and one in Gilroy and one in Seaside. Luke was the leader of a group of bikers as a front, and he rode.

Luke, in Oscar's eyes, was the perfect target for him to move out. If he could get Luke out the way he could take over. He thought he could move into San Francisco within a year if things went right. That was his plan, but he needed a package.

He formed a plan to take over a trap house and see what Luke did. So, Oscar walked into the trap house and shot the two guy's in it and took the drugs and money. Three crackheads witnessed the shooting from across the street. Oscar left them to tell Luke's people the story. He yelled, as he left the house driving off, that he ran this street now, and if they were buying crack, that he was the boss now.

He waited to see what Luke was going to do, but nothing happened. Luke didn't come at him or even send anyone at him. He just took it in the ass and moved on.

From that moment, Oscar knew as soon as he saw Luke on the streets, he was going to kill him. Then he would have the whole pie. Even the biker's from Merced had not stepped to him.

＊＊

Chapter 31

Flip had been looking for Oscar while he was being hunted himself. Seemed his boss wanted him dead for his failure to kill Nicholas. He was now in Cali, a state he hated, and in a town, he knew little about.

He could not go to any of the people he knew for fear of his whereabouts getting back to the boss. So, he was on his own, he had to get Oscar and somehow finish the job on Nicholas.

He decided that he was going to find out where they had taken Nicholas. His plan was to finish the job. Finding Nicholas was the easy part. He got in contact with an old Doctor in Oaktown he knew. The doctor told him Nicholas' Doctor, was Doctor David T. Logan, Head of Medicine at Alameda hospital. A very private hospital located in Alameda, CA. Doctor Logan had his practice there and did most of his surgeries there.

Turned out that he was right. When Flip went to the hospital, he spotted the two men driving around the block and the two in the lobby. He posed as an orderly to gain access to the patient's floors. He saw two men guarding a private room. He notices that only one nurse was allowed to go into the room. He saw that the other three rooms on that side of the floor were empty, and that all the other activity was on the other side of the nurse's station.

At the cafeteria, he was able to learn Nicholas had private nurses hired by Doctor Logan from an agency. He then devised a plan. His plan was to replace one of the nurses with his own person, but how was he going to do it? He was still thinking it through when it dawned on him, if only the nurses could enter Nicholas room without question from the guards, he couldn't take a chance on doing it himself, too big of a risk that someone would recognize him.

He left the hospital and called Mexico, to a woman who did some work in Houston for him. He hoped she had not been in contact with anyone in Houston and was not working for the boss.

Juanita Lopez called (El Scorpion) on the streets was a hit woman with a great deal of skills. She was a cold-hearted killer. Her first kill was at the age of ten when she killed her father and brother for raping her. She did nine hard years in jail, and then was released back into the streets of Veracruz, Mexico.

Juanita was an unbelievably beautiful woman who learned to use her body as a weapon, and to use the skills of being a nurse in prison, where she was an assistant to Doctors. Flip got Juanita to kill a local politician about a year ago who was in the hospital, and it worked out great, so he thought he could do the same thing here.

Flip promised her fifty thousand for the job. Twenty out front and the rest after she was done. She was happy to get the money because she was in debt with a local gangster in Veracruz for her cocaine habit. She knew how to play her role, and she knew how to be a nurse; but mainly she liked to kill people.

Flip got her set up to move into the day nurse's place. The young nurse left her apartment in Hayward at five for work, walked to her car in the parking lot and she was shot in the head. Her dead body was placed in the trunk and the car locked.

Juanita took her place that morning and nobody thought anything about it. When Doctor Logan saw her, he asked if she was sent by the agency, and she replied, "yes". He was so busy that he didn't think anything about checking up on her.

***

Nina and Vivian where walking toward Nick's room, when Nina noticed that the nurse, at the nurse's station, was different. The nurse didn't seem right to her. Something inside Nina's head was telling her to check out the nurse. She had not asked to change nurse's or replace anyone, and she wanted to ask Nick's Doctor why the other nurse was replaced.

Doctor Logan said that it was not unusual for the agency to change a nurse. Sometimes they had a special skill and that they were needed elsewhere, and they would change nurses. He said he was sure it was okay. Nina was not happy and told Vivian she didn't like the nurse. Nina thought the nurse was foul and she was going to watch her. Nina went to the point of telling the two guards to watch her.

"This nurse is not to be left alone with Nick. I want one of you to be in the room with her at all times, understand", said Nina, to the guards.

***

Chapter 32

Today, Hazel and Nicholas Jr. were sitting down with the bankers and lawyers, to finalize negotiating the contract sale of Bay Side Savings and Loan Association to Simmons Incorporated.

Hazel was the chief accountant for Simmons Inc., while Nicholas Jr. was there to sit in for his stepmother, Nina, who was recovering from a car accident.

The lawyers for both sides had skillfully and fairly negotiated and litigated most of the terms of the sale. Today's meeting was just a formality of going over some minor terms before submitting the final sale to the banking commission for approval. The government was set to transfer all savings and loan companies to full-service banks, with the next vote in congress.

By the end of the meeting, Nicholas Jr., realized just how smart his stepmother Nina was. She had successfully gotten a savings and loan to sell over 85% of their stock to Simmons Inc. for a cash infusion and buyout.

After the meeting, JR and Hazel went by the house to tell Nina how the meeting went. They brought her up to speed, while they ate a late lunch on the patio out by the pool. Hazel, Vivian, JR, and Nina sat there enjoying the fresh crab and shrimp with a white wine sauce, while drinking a cabernet from Napa. They played cards, sat and talked. Nina let them know Nicholas was still in a coma and that Doctor Logan said Nicholas was having some more plastic surgery on his face tomorrow.

***

Every day, Nina, along with Vivian or Maria came to the hospital to see Nick. She had a florist deliver fresh flowers every morning. The first week she had to be wheeled in because of the brace. She would roll her wheelchair up to the bed and sit there talking to Nick for hours. Some day's Vivian or Maria would leave her there and come back in a couple of hours to take her home. Every day without failure, she was there sitting and talking to Nicholas, telling him to come back to her, because she needed him.

Now she was able to walk a little better but could only wear tennis shoes, she hated tennis shoes for anything other than the gym but didn't have any flats. Her heels made her neck hurt, when she tried to where them...... Vivian told her to wear her house shoes, but she didn't like to wear those soft, open toed shoes, because they didn't have any support. She decided that she and Vivian were going to get some comfortable flats sometime today.

While she was sitting there, the day nurse walked in and looked at Nick's chart. It was just something about the woman that rubbed Nina the wrong way. She didn't trust the woman. The nurse had done nothing to Nina for her to feel that way, it was just the way she looked and acted when Nina was around that had her on edge. Nina had asked Doctor Logan about the nurse a couple of times and he had stated that she was good.

Doctor Logan told Nina that he was taking Nick off the medicine, which caused him to remain in the chemically induced coma. That he expected him to start to wake up in the next few days. That news caused Nina so much joy and happiness, she pushed the nurse to the back burner of her thoughts.

She talked to Nick and told him about the meeting with the bankers and that she hoped to get word that the deal was approved. After an hour, Vivian walked in and told her she needed to go, because she had an appointment with her doctor at two and it was one. So, she said her good-byes and kissed Nick on the lips.

***

Having left Nina's doctor appointment about 3:30 and not wanting to just go to the house, Nina and Vivian decided they were going to go shopping for flat shoes. Walking in high heels was too uncomfortable and Nina didn't want to keep wearing tennis shoes with regular clothes.

Besides, she wanted to get out and enjoy the rest of the day, doing something fun. Lately, all she had been doing was going to the hospital to see how Nicholas was doing and needed a girl's day out.

She decided they would go to I. Magnin, in Union Square, San Francisco, and then have lunch at a little Chinese restaurant in the financial district. After parking at the O'Farrell Street Garage, Vivian and Nina crossed the street and walked into Macy's, which had a pass through to I. Magnin, making their way to the shoe department.

A friendly salesman approached them and said, "Good afternoon ladies, how may I help you?", in a very professional manner.

"I would like to try on some walking sandals, soft leather, in all the colors you have," said Nina, in a curious but nonchalant voice.

"Well ladies, you are in for a very pleasant surprise, we just got a new shipment. A new style that came from Italy just a couple of days ago. And your size?" "Please bring me a size 6½ and a 7.

The salesman left and went to get the shoes. While waiting, Nina noticed the woman sitting across from them. Not because she was black but because she seemed out of place and was talking loudly. She keeps telling the sales woman helping her that she needed a wider size and kept cussing at the woman.

But what got Nina's attention was the woman waving her left hand, and on it was Nina's grandmother's ring, which came up missing from her stuff at the hospital.

"That bitch has my ring on her left hand," said Nina, to Vivian, in a low deadly voice.

"What you say? I didn't hear you," replied Vivian. "See that woman right there... She has my ring, the blue sapphire and diamond ring I had in my purse the night of the shooting. The one the hospital claimed they didn't have or hadn't seen. "They claimed it wasn't on my property slip," said Nina, loud enough for Vivian to hear her clearly.

Vivian remembered Nina wearing the ring many times, and the story behind it. She looked at the woman and saw the ring, Vivian remembered the woman, then she turned to Nina and said, "that bitch works at the hospital. She's the nurse that was in the emergency room. I remember her from when we got there that night. She must have took it out of the property bag along with your money," stated Vivian, with a cold stare.

"Yeah, well I'm going to get it back and get in her ass," replied Nina, sounding a bit angry and upset.

"Let's follow her out of here and confront her at her car. Girl, you up to the walk and getting in her ass?" "I got the strength, and I'm real motivated to get my ring back."

"Ladies, here are the newest styles we have," stated the salesman, as he sits on the stool in front of Nina, so she could try on the flats.

She tried on one pair in a 7 and was satisfied with the fit. Keeping her eye on the woman who had her ring, told the salesman to ring them up on her account, in all the available colors, and deliver them to her address.

Nina and Vivian waited for the woman to pay for the shoes that she bought and followed her to the parking lot. The woman had parked on the fifth floor and took the elevator up. Nina and Vivian got on the elevator right behind her and rode up to the fifth floor. Nina had her 380 automatic in her right hand and Vivian had hers in her left hand as the doors to the elevator opened. Nina put her gun in the woman's left side, and said, "walk to your car and don't say a word."

"Vivian was on the other side of the woman and had her gun in the woman's ribs on the right side. The woman was so afraid that she peed on herself, scared and shaking from fear.

"What... I haven't done anything to you...Please don't hurt me, take the money and leave me alone," she begged, with tears in her eyes.

When they got to her little car, a Ford focus, Nina told her to get in the back seat while Vivian walked around and got in the front seat.

"Take that ring off and hand it to me... How the fuck you going to steal from me?" Nina said, and started to hit her in the face with the gun but stopped short of hitting her.

The woman took the ring off and handed it to Nina, while saying, "Please don't kill me, I didn't mean..." Nina cut her off "shut the fuck up and listen. I know who you are, where you live and where you work. If I hear of you talking to anyone about this, I will finish the job and your family will wear their best black...Understand what I'm saying to you bitch?", Nina said, with a cold hard stare with hate in her eyes.

"Yes...Yes I understand... I will never take anything again... I just...I didn't mean to..." Shut up! I don't want to hear it."

Nina hit the woman with the butt of the gun on the side of her face knocking her out cold in the back seat of her car. Vivian was watching for any passer-by that might see something they didn't need to see. They got out of the car and took the elevator down to the third floor, back to Vivian's car, got in and headed out of the garage. They drove to the Chinese restaurant for lunch and talked about the woman they left unconscious at the garage.

***

When Vivian got in from her outing with Nina, she found Tyrone sitting in his big chair watching the Raider game. "How was your day," asked Tyrone, "and how is baby girl"?

"We had a good time, but we had an incident happen while in I. Magnin," replied Vivian.

"What the hell happened," asked Tyrone.

"We were in the shoe department and Nina recognized her grandmother's ring on this woman's finger, and I remembered her from the hospital, the night of the shooting. She was the nurse on duty, and Nina's cash came up missing as well. We figured she was guilty as hell and decided to follow her out the store and get the ring back."

"She had parked in the garage on O'Farrell on the 5th floor, so we took the elevator up to where she got off and confronted her at her car. Nina and I were both strapped and had a gun pressed into both her sides. Nina was ready to whop that ass, but we just forced her into the back seat and told her to take off the ring.

She was pissing and crying the whole time, scared to death; not the nasty person people met at the hospital. She gave up the ring and was apologizing so hard, Nina told her to shut the fuck up."

"Then what happened, did anyone see you"?

"We threatened her and told her we knew where she lived and where she worked. Nina pistol whipped her, knocked her out, and we left her unconscious in her back seat.

Nobody else was on that floor at the time we fucked her up, and I didn't see any cameras."

"Damn, you and Nina really got gangster and handled that shit," said Tyrone, while thinking, "it's a loose end that needs to be dealt with."

Vivian went upstairs while Tyrone made a call to Charles. "Hey man, this is Tyrone, need you to make a problem go away."

"When do you need me," answered Charles.

"Now," barked Tyrone, "meet me at Merritt Bakery in the parking lot and I'll give you the info."

"Solid, my man, be there in 30 minutes", replied Charles, and hung up. Charles left the house to meet with Tyrone and get his instructions.

The next morning Charles went to the hospital and found that the nurse on duty was the one he came to get. Finding out that her shift ended at 9 o'clock, he returned to the hospital just in time to see her walk out the building, into the garage to her Ford focus. He walked up to the car, pulled his 9mm and blew the back of her head off. He turned and walked away and left the area; it was a silent and ruthless kill.

***

Chapter 33

William had spent the last week hiding in the motel, waiting for Carl to finish the passport and new licenses for him and Susan. Carl had got picked up for being under the Influence, a judge gave him five days and fined him one-hundred and fifty. William had to wait for his papers, so he could not go out because word on the streets was Tyrone was looking for him.

Just this morning Carl called and told him he was bringing the papers through. William was so excited about getting the papers, it meant he could get the hell out of this hell hole.

His plan was to drive to Sacramento, then take a plane to Portland or Seattle, where he could get on a ship and go to Portugal. His family had property in Portugal where he would be safe. Susan just wanted to get the hell out of the motel. She was sick of the smell of onions coming from the fields. Sick of the hot dogs, hamburgers, and chicken wings with pizza, they had been eating for now going on two weeks.

"When Carl gets here, be packed so we can leave", stated William, trying to sound confident.

"Yeah, it's about damn time... I'll be happy to leave this place", replied Susan.

"Yeah, let's make sure you got the bags in the car, Carl said he'd be here in about an hour."

"What bags are you talking about... everything's in the car, we only got two bags."

"Shut the fuck up and go watch the television and leave me alone."

It was after three when Carl Knocked on the door, almost scaring William out of his pants. Susan jumped at the sound of the door like she was a little kid, and something scared her. As William reached for his gun laying on the table next to the bed, he eased up to the door.

"Who is it", he said, in a nervous voice.

127

"It's me, Carl, let me in."

"Opening the door just wide enough to point his gun out, he pointed it at the side of Carl's head. William then opened the door a little wider and looked around the courtyard. He was looking to see if anyone was with Carl. Seeing no one, he let Carl in, locked the door and looked at the courtyard again through the window.

"You got the papers", asked William?

"First, you got my money?"

"Yeah, I got it, right there in that case."

"Well, let me see the money and I will let you see the papers."

"Susan, show him the money", said William, while he stayed by the door.

Susan walked over to the table, got the case and opened it so Carl could see in it. Carl looked at all the hundred's and fifty's and his eyes got big. He took a package from under his coat out and handed it to William. As Susan gave him the case, William walked over to the counter and opened the package and looked at the passports, social security cards, licenses and birth certificates for him and Susan. He shook his head, while saying, damn you're good. I can't tell the difference from real documents.

"I'm the best", said Carl, as he started to the door.

"Well, thanks for the papers and your help, I would say I'll be seeing you, but I'm not."

Carl stopped dead in his tracks. "What do you mean?"

"Oh, I just mean I will not be around, so we will not see each other", said William, as he unlocked the door and let Carl leave.

Once Carl had left, William turned to Susan and said, "let's get the fuck up out of here."

Nicholas II A Storm is Coming

"How about we go to the Cattlemen's up the road and eat a good meal before we leave. I'm dying for some good food, something other than Hamburgers or pizza", said Susan, with a little attitude.

"They don't open until five, what time is it?"

"Oh, it's four-thirty and by the time we drive there and buy gas to get us to Seattle, it will be five."

"That works for me, let's go", said William, full of joy because he was getting out of Cali and thought he was getting away from Tyrone's hand.

***

Frank and his girl were on their way to Reno, to have a little fun and make some money. Now driving up highway 80 towards Sacramento, his girl wanted to stop at the Cattleman's, she had heard from other's that their food was the bomb... she wanted to stop and eat. She really wanted to buy a souvenir that she could show her girlfriends back home, leaving the ghetto was a big deal for them.

They were hood rats and would probably never leave the county limits. Their idea of success was getting a dope boy and having a baby. Olivia wanted to get out of the lower bottom, she wanted to move up in the Hills. She was trying her best to make Frank a better man, trying to teach him some class and how to be more sophisticated and cultured. If it were up to Frank, he would eat chicken wings and fast food every day.

They got to the restaurant and were seated in the main dining room in a booth. Frank was nervous, he was out of his element. He was unsure of how to act, he didn't like white people and right now, he was in the midst of a bunch. He kept his head on a swivel and tried to make a good impression on Olivia. He really cared for her and was happy that she was having his baby. If everything went right, he planned to marry her, but right now he was on a mission.

The waiter walked up to the table "good evening... welcome to the cattlemen's... is this your first visit with us?", he asked Frank, in a friendly voice.

"Yes, yes, this is our first time, what do you suggest?", asked Olivia.

"Everything we have is exceptionally good, maybe you'll want to take a moment and look at the menu".

"Yes, let's look at the menu", said Frank, trying to sound proper.

"OK, I'll get your drinks while you look over the menu. Would you like to order any wine?

"I'd like a CC and water and bring the lady a Virgin Margarita".

"Very well... let me get your drinks... while you look at the menu and I'll be back in a few moments, enjoy yourself".

With that, the waiter walked off to get the drinks. Frank was still nervous and was looking around the room. In his mind, he thought everyone was looking at him. The place was much larger than it looked from the road. It was about half full, but there were lots of people coming in.

The Cattleman's was immensely popular, one of the most popular restaurants on Hwy 80. People coming from Oakland, and the city, going to Sacramento or to Reno or Tahoe, would stop here to eat. Those coming from Sacramento to the Bay Area, would stop in and have a bite.

Unknown to Frank, William pulled into the gas station and filled up his Mercedes. He wanted to buy gas, so if he weren't able to catch a plane, he could drive to Oregon or on up to Seattle. Williams knew he wasn't going to stay in Sacramento, it wasn't safe. After filling the car, he pulled over into the Cattlemen's parking lot, where Susan and he got out the car and walked into the Cattleman's.

"Good evening, welcome to the Cattleman's," said the hostess, with a country accent.

"Two for dinner, said William, with a smile on his face.

"Yes sir, it will be about ten minutes before a table will be ready. May I have a name that I may page you by?" asked the hostess, with a smile.

"William" ... We will be in the bar... Thank you", said William.

"Very well sir... I'll have your waiter come get you when your table is ready."

With that, William took Susan by the arm and guided her to the bar.

"May I have a JB water back...please", said William, when the bartender placed two napkins in front of him and Susan.

"And for the lady?", asked the bartender

"She will have a Screwdriver," replied William.

Susan was busy looking at the country memorabilia and décor. She'd only been to the Cattleman's once before and then she didn't really pay attention to the decor. The bartender fixed their drinks and placed them on the napkin. They sat at the bar drinking their drinks, waiting for their table. About ten minutes passed before a young waiter walked up, "excuse me, Mr. Williams, your table is ready, follow me please, leave your drinks, I will have them brought to your table."

The waiter turned and walked away, he led them into the main dining area. He took them to a booth, which was directly across from where Frank and Olivia were sitting. Susan sat on one side and William sat facing the door. Their drinks were brought from the bar and the waiter asked, "would you like a moment to look over the menu...I can have your drinks refreshed if you like."

"That'll be fine young man", said William.

The waiter then walked away. William asked Susan, "How do you like the place?"

"I like it a lot, I hope the food is good", said Susan, anticipating eating a good meal. Anything had to be better than the food she been eating for the past two weeks.

"I'm looking forward to a good rib eye steak, and a fully loaded potato, said William.

"I see here on the menu, that they serve pork chops. I think I'll have pork chops with some mixed vegetables", said Susan.

When the waiter returned, they placed their order, and then continued to talk, making their plans for the future.

***

Frank, looking around, spotted William, and could not believe his eyes. He took a hard look at William and Susan and almost lost it. He got a hold of his emotions, trying to slow his heartbeat down, as it started to race.

"Hey babe, look, I just saw that dude that I'm supposed to be looking for. He's sitting over there in that booth across from us. I have to call Tyrone, so I'm going out to the phone booth, you just wait here."

"Hey, babe is that safe? What if he spots you... Or he starts shooting ... what you want me to do? You know I got your back", said Olivia, while her blood pressure was going through the roof.

"No, you just sit here and finish eating. He is not going to start anything in this place. I will be careful...He will not see me. He doesn't even know me from the man in the moon. So just chill... I'm going to call Tyrone and get some help.

With that said, Frank went to the phone booth, which was out front and called Tyrone.

***

The phone rang three times before Tyrone was able to answer. He placed the phone to his ear and listened.

"Hello, may I speak to Tyrone? This is Frank", said Frank, into the phone.

"Hey young blood what's happening?", answered Tyrone.

"I just... I mean me and my girl are up here at the Cattlemen's off highway 880, eating... I just saw that dude William. He came in to eat. What do you want me to do?"

132

"Wait a minute, slow down, you saw William at the Cattlemen's."

"Yeah, he's inside eating right now."

"Can you keep him there until I can get there?"

"Yeah, I can do that once he leaves out. I think it will be a minute. He and his bitch just got here, and the place is packed, so he may be here for an hour or two."

"Just hold him, and Frank, don't shoot him... Just hold on to him. I'll be there as fast as I can get there."

"Okay, I'll hold him and his bitch".

"Hey, what car are you in?"

"I'm driving the firebird."

"See you in a few", said Tyrone, and hung up the phone. He quickly picked it up again and called Roland.

***

Roland answered the phone on the second ring, "Talk to me."

"Hey Roland, get to my house, and bring Charles, we have some business to take care of."

"I'm on the way boss, see you in about ten."

As he ended the call, Tyrone got up and walked into the bedroom to change clothes. Taking a pair of black wool slacks and a long black sleeve silk shirt from the closet and putting them on. He took his black leather shoulder holster and the extra clip, slipped his chrome 45 into the holster and grabbing two extra clips, he then placed a 9mm in the belt holster in his lower back.

V had been in the bedroom resting and sat up in the bed while Tyrone was in the closet. She got up and walked into the closet.

"What's up, where are you going?"

"I just got a call from Frank, the young dude from down in the Village. Seems

he found William up in Dixon at the Cattlemen's. I'm headed up there to take hold of him. Frank is keeping him there, until I get up there. Don't wait up, I may be late getting in tonight."

"Okay, you be careful out there and don't get hurt, I love you."

She walked into his arms and planted a kiss on his face and lips. He was an O.G., but he was putty in her hands. He wanted to say I love you too, but he was hard, and it just did not sound right coming out his mouth, but he said, "me too."

Roland pulled up in his new Lincoln town car with Charles riding shotgun. Tyrone got in the back and told them to head for Dixon, as quick as possible. Roland hit the freeway, doing over 80 headed towards the Sacramento area.

***

Meanwhile, back at the Cattlemen's, Frank returned to his table and told Olivia the deal. Their food had come while he was on the phone and Olivia was busy eating her food and didn't really want to talk.

"Go ahead baby, and eat while you can", she said, as she placed a fork full of potatoes in her mouth.

Frank cut into the rib eye steak and took a bite, as he chewed the tender beef, he kept one eye on the booth across the room. He could see that William had ordered, but their food had not come. William and Susan were talking and drinking. They seemed to be so engrossed in their conversation that they didn't care about anyone else around them.

He thought to himself, "what if William got up to leave, would he be able to hold them in the parking lot. He wondered if William was holding, because Tyrone wanted him alive, he hoped he didn't get in a shootout."

As he continued to eat his food, he saw the waitress bring William's order and realized that he was going to be there for a minute eating.

Nicholas II A Storm is Coming

He sat back in the booth, eased the 45 from his waistband out, and checked the clip, jacking one into the chamber and placed the safety on. He placed it back in his waistband.

Having finished his meal, and toying with a piece of chocolate cake for dessert, he watched as William and the woman continued to eat and talk. About twenty minutes went by and suddenly William looked up from the table and scanned the room, using his hand to call for his waitress.

"May I have the check?", said William, to the waiter, who was passing by...

"Yes sir, I will have your waiter bring it to you right away."

The waiter placed the check on the table and told William he would be the cashier for him. William, without looking at the check, placed a one hundred-dollar bill on the check and said, "Thank you, the food was good."

The waiter looked at the money and smiled because the check was only eighty-five dollars. "Thank you, sir, did you leave room for dessert? Or do you want to take some dessert to go?"

"No, I'm stuffed, and I have a long drive ahead."

Frank was watching from the booth and told Olivia to get ready to leave. He placed a hundred on the table for their meal, got up and headed to the front door, beating William out so he could catch him coming out.

Olivia ran to Frank's firebird and pulled it to the front side of the restaurant parking lot, so she could see the front door and Frank. Frank placed himself in the waiting area knowing William would have to come out that way.

It'd been just over an hour since he called Tyrone, Frank knew it would take anywhere from an hour to an hour and a half to get to Dixon, and he was wondering what he would do if William came out before Tyrone got there.

Being a public place, where could he put two people, knowing his firebird didn't have a big back seat area? As he was thinking, the door opened, and William and the woman walked out. Frank eased up behind him, putting his 45 in his rib cage and told him.

"Don't make a sound, don't try to run, shut up and walk to your car, without making a scene, or I will blow your back out... now move."

William was so shocked that he almost peed on himself, Susan wanted to scream. Frank said, "If you do, it'll be the last thing you or he hears."

Some way she stopped the scream in midair, her mouth open but no sound came out. They started towards the parking space where William was parked. Frank walked between them like he was their friend while holding the gun in the ribs of William's right side.

Olivia saw him and pulled into the parking space next to William and got out, she walked up to Frank and took hold of Susan and walked with her. Olivia placed her 380 automatic in Susan's back and told her to walk.

They both were watching to see if any bystanders were looking. The car was only fifty feet from the front door, so Frank was a little concerned that someone would see him.

"Open the door, you got any guns on you?", Frank asked, as he patted down William with his left hand.

"No, I don't have a gun, why are you doing this?", said William, with a great deal of concern in his voice.

"Shut the fuck up and get in the back seat," Frank said, as he pointed the gun at him. Olivia pushed Susan into the back seat of the Benz. William told Frank a 9mm was in the glove compartment. Frank hit William in the head with the butt of his gun. William felt the blow and the blood that rushed out the top of his head.

"I asked you if you had any guns, motherfucker, and you said no. Now get the fuck in the car. Frank looked for any bystander that may have been looking as he pushed William into the back seat.

Nicholas II A Storm is Coming

"Baby, watch them while I get a roll of tape out my trunk. Better yet, you go look in my trunk and get that big roll of duct tape", said Frank, to Olivia, who got out and got the duct tape and handed it to Frank. While she held her gun on William and Susan, Frank tied their hands and feet with the duct tape. He and Olivia sat in the front seat waiting and looking for Tyrone.

He decided to move the Benz from the front to the back of the lot. He told Olivia to drive his car to the back of the parking lot, facing the freeway. With Susan and William duct taped in the back seat he drove the Benz to the back.

**

Frank spotted Roland's town car turning into the parking lot and blinked the lights on the Benz to get his attention. Roland pulled right next to the Benz and parked. He and Charles jumped out; Charles opened the rear door for Tyrone to get out.

William looked out the window at the three men approaching the back of the Mercedes and wished he were dreaming. Outside, headed his way was the one man in this world, he didn't want to see.

Tyrone was walking towards him with the coldest stare and blank eyes that showed no emotion or remorse. He appeared to be even harder than the streets had said, like he was not even alive. He was like something in a movie. Death walked in his shoes and William knew his time had come. "Well now, look what we have here, it's been a minute, but I got you now."

"Wait... wait a minute... what do you want with me?", William said, with fear in his voice.

"I want to talk to you?" Tyrone said.

**

137

Chapter 34

Roland drove to the ranch, with William and Susan tied up in the trunk, he pulled around to the shed. When he opened the trunk, the smell of shit and piss rushed out, inflaming his nostrils. "What the fuck, you nasty motherfucker, you shit in my car... I ought to shoot you right here," said Roland, with a totally disgusted look in his eye.

"You are a fucked-up Individual."

Once in the shed, he re-tied them using some rope. When Charles arrived the first thing that Charles said was, "What is that stinking smell...It smells like someone has died up in here." Charles was in his usual dark and somewhat grim mood.

Tyrone knew the smell all too well. It was the smell of death. It was the smell of others who had sat in that shed and never left alive. William and Susan were to be the next to meet the Grim Reaper.

Tyrone walked into the shed and said, "well now William Franklin, I heard tell you like to shoot people," in a chilling voice that made the hair on Charles' arm rise. Roland thought to himself, "*I hope I never get on the bad side of Tyrone.*"

William was scared shitless and you could see the fear in his eyes. "Please don't kill me, please let me go," his eyes begged. William wanted to talk but the rag in his mouth prevented any sound. Roland reached down pulling the rag out of his mouth, immediately William started begging and crying, "I didn't shoot him....I didn't shoot him, all I did was drive the van. Please take pity on me, have mercy... I'll give you... I'll give you everything I got. You can have all my money, just let me live, just let me leave."

"I don't need your money, I need information. I want the ones who sent you, because I know you're not the brains behind this, but you're going to tell me who sent you."

"I don't know anything; I was given eighty thousand to pay the two hitters and to drive the van."

Nicholas II A Storm is Coming

"Who told you? That's what I wanna know, who sent you to shoot Nicholas? It's a simple question that requires a simple answer, but let's take this to the next level."

"I told you I don't know... I was only the money man". William screamed when the hammer hit his foot and smashed two of his toes.

"Now I'll ask again, who sent you?", said Tyrone, with no pity in his voice.

"A woman named Carmella brought me the eighty thousand and told me to pay the two hitters when the job was done. Please don't kill me."

"Once again, you don't get it, I want the names."

And the hammer came down again on William's foot as the other two toes were smashed and blood shot over the floor. The pain was so great that William tried to pass out, but Tyrone was not having that, he slapped William across the face to wake him up.

While this was happening, Susan, who was sitting in a chair, hearing the sounds of pain, and was scared to death. Wishing she had left William before all of this started, now she thought she was going to die behind something that William did. The money she had taken from William was not worth her life, but she didn't know anything, she was just a gold digger, trying to get over.

William looked at Tyrone and realized he was going to tell him everything, maybe then Tyrone would let him live. "I can tell you the two who set up Nicholas, and the two hitters who did the shooting, with tears running down his face and pain so great he could hardly talk.

He started with the two who got the information on Nicholas, "it was P-Slim and his partner Dirty Mike. They are from Oaktown, the hitters were Oscar and Juan, they were from Houston, Texas. They work for a dealer named Phillip Haynes, known on the streets as Flip," said William, rambling through the pain.

Tyrone picked up a burning piece of wood from the barrel and placed it on Williams leg. William screamed and shit on his self from the pain. That really pissed Tyrone off and he took the still burning piece of wood and placed it on the side of his face, burning him to the bone.

After an hour of questions and more torture, getting the same answer over and over again, Tyrone was satisfied that William had given all he had to give.

"Take him out and feed the hogs", said Tyrone, as he turned and walked toward Susan's chair.

Roland and Charles did as they were told and removed William from the chair. "You want us to shoot him, before we put him in the pen", asked Charles.

"No, why shoot him… we are going to feed him to the hogs alive", replied Roland.

"What do you want? I have money, I can pay you to let me go", asked Susan, as Tyrone approached her chair. She thought by giving Tyrone money, he would let her go.

Tyrone looked at Susan and thought to himself, *"this shit is getting crazy."* He took out a cigarette, lit it, and took a big draw from it, blowing out a ring of smoke into the air.

He walked around the chair, looked down, and said, "Now tell me who sent you? Don't talk, and you force me to make you talk by hurting you. Pain you have never thought about in your young life. I will make you feel pain and hurt in places that you don't want to know about. Do you understand yet that this is not a game and I do not plan to be nice? Now talk because you are going to tell me what I want to know."

***

P-Slim and Dirty Mike had gotten the money from William at the bait shop. They both had five thousand. P-Slim was going to stay low, he planned to use the FBI and DEA for some protection. After all, he was an undercover CI for the FBI and DEA. They allowed him to stay on the streets as long as he provided them information on dealers and shipments. He didn't comprehend that when you ran afoul of Tyrone, nothing could stop him or the storm that was coming your way.

Dirty-Mike on the other hand, took his money and got the hell out of town. He went to Bakersfield to hide. He was not going to hang around taking a chance that Tyrone would not find him. He took a greyhound bus to Bakersfield, leaving his car on a side street. The plan may have worked, if not for the fact that a crackhead saw him get on the bus.

Two days after getting the money from William, Paul Collins, aka P-Slim, got busted for Intent to sale. The FBI was holding him in Greystone to await trial. They placed him in protective custody, isolated him from other inmates. However, P-Slim could not remain cool, true to his foolish pride and big mouth, he had to prove he was a big man. He started talking about how he did this, and how he did that in the streets. His mouth was running all the time. He had money on the books and could buy commissary at the canteen, so he was able to keep up his front.

***

Chapter 35

Nicholas has been in a chemically induced coma for four weeks. His body was healing well; however, his mind was far from resting, it was hard at work. He was alive and not dead, or at least he didn't believe he was dead, because he could hear Nina talking and praying. He heard people talking but he could not open his eyes or raise his hand, but he could hear them. For some reason, he could hear and understand what they were saying, but he could not answer. He would just drift off into a deep sleep and dream. Sometimes he could make out the dreams but most of the time he just drifted. He was trying to wake up from this nightmare but every time he tried to open his eyes, he couldn't. He continued to struggle to open his eyes.

***

Word had gotten out that William had gotten killed by Tyrone. The fact of the matter is the streets didn't know for sure. Word was William was shot by Tyrone up in Portland. Other's said, he was food for the fish in the bay, while still others said, he was cut up and fed to the lions at the Oakland Zoo. The streets don't always get the facts right, but they did know that William was gone.

***

Struggling now to open his eye's, coming out of the deep fog, Nicholas could barely see the light. He tried to focus his eyes; the room was dark, and he could not raise his arm or move his head. However, he could see the light above him. Nicholas tried to talk and found that his voice was not there.

The night nurse, a bright young male nurse walked in and saw him trying to move, ran to his side, and began to help him.

"Now, Mr. Simmons, careful, you are okay, just take it easy. You have been asleep for a while and need to slow down."

"Try to just lay there and rest a moment, I will help you," he said.

"Do you want some water?" he asked and held his hand.

Nicholas tried once again to speak, "yes" but he did not hear the words.

"Here you go" as he placed the straw in his mouth, and Nicholas sucked a little. John picked up the phone, next to the bed, pulled out a piece of paper with a number on it from his pocket and dialed it.

"Hello", said the soft voice on the phone.

"Hello, this is John, the nurse at Alameda Hospital, am I speaking to Mrs. Simmons?", he asked.

"Yes," came the reply from Nina, with a bit of concern.

"He is awake, your husband, Mr. Simmons just woke up," he told her.

"Oh my God, thank you, I will be right there," Nina said, jumping up so fast that she felt a sharp pain in her neck. She was so excited; she couldn't worry about her own pain.

Nick was awake, she had to get to the hospital. Now she hadn't driven herself since she got home, but she was going to get to that hospital right now. She grabbed the pager typing in 0909 and sent it to all. It was code that Nick was awake. She called for a cab and told the man to hurry.

***

Tyrone looked at his pager, saw 0909, jumped up, and looked at Vivian, as her pager was going off also. They started to the garage without a word. They arrived at the hospital just as Nina was getting out of a cab. Tyrone let Vivian out the car at the curb, next to where Nina was standing, then pulled off to find a place to park, while Nina and Vivian went in.

Inside the hospital, Nina and Vivian were coming out the elevator, when they saw Nick's Doctor. Doctor Logan was coming out of Nickels room as they turned the corner.

"Doctor Logan how is he doing," Nina asked, as she walked up to the doctor.

"Oh, hello there, he is doing well, he is awake, and his signs are great. He still has the feeding tube, but John is removing it now, and will start him on ice chips for now. I'm taking him off the morphine drip and I will write a prescription, for Norco, a pain pill that is less addictive. However, he may still have to go to physical therapy, to learn how to use all his extremities.

His memory may have suffered some loss, but it should come back in time. But all things considered, I'd say he's doing very well. I'll check on him again later in the morning. How are you doing... How are you feeling?" reaching down and looking at her neck.

"I see you're healing very well, so let me go and start making the arrangements to get him some physical therapy and get him into one of the psychological training sessions. You have a good day, I'll be talking to you soon", said Doctor Logan, who turned and started to walk away.

"Thank you", replied Nina, as she ran into Nickels' room.

Nickels was laying in the bed and John the nurse was removing the feeding tube from his throat. It was extremely uncomfortable and hurt as the nurse removed the feeding tube.

"Hold still now", the nurse said, as he eased the tube out.

"Nickels, baby please be still and let him do his work", Nina said, like a mother talking to a child.

Nickels just cut his eyes over at her, as he laid there feeling the tube being pulled out of his throat. Nickels was in pain and wanted to tell all of them to kiss his ass. However, he knew they were trying to help.

The nurse finished removing the tube and started to clean him up. He got the sheets and pillows right, letting Nick layback on the pillows to get comfortable. He handed Nick some ice chips to suck on to ease the sore feeling in his mouth and throat. Nick had to admit the ice did feel good and the cool taste helped the soreness in his mouth.

Nicholas II A Storm is Coming

Nick tried to talk to Nina, to tell her how happy he was to see her, and how much he loved her. However, the words would not come out. He still had the bandages around his mouth and face from the operation on his jaw bone.

He just laid there and looked at her. Nina ran and jumped on the edge of the bed, as she grabbed him by the head and started kissing him tenderly on the lips. She was placing kisses all over his head.

Vivian just stood there and watched along with the two bodyguards. Tyrone walked up, seeing Nickels was awake, and that Nina was making a fuss, he fell back and just watched.

What he needed to do was clear and he had a mission. Vivian saw him standing outside the room, walked to him, and told him, what the doctor said. Tyrone looked down at her and smiled, "I knew he would come out of it. Now we have to get him home safe, then find the one who caused this mess."

***

B ack at home Nina was appreciative that Nickels was woke. She now needed to make sure he was completely out of harm's way. Seeing they still didn't know who had orchestrated the hit. However, she knew if they found out he was alive, they would be coming.

She always had a gun near. She thought about all the times Nickels had made her go to the ranch to shoot. How he drilled into her to shoot at the stomach not the head. She had never shot anyone, but if it came down to saving her life or his, she was damn sure it would not be a problem.

She checked all the doors and windows in the house and set the security systems and got in bed. She checked the clip in her beretta 380 and placed it beside her on the nightstand. After praying for everyone and thanking God for allowing Nickels to return to her, she closed her eyes and fell asleep.

***

The next morning Nina called Nicholas' sons, telling them to come to the house right away. She wanted to let them know that their father was awake. When they got to the house, she told them that he was awake, but still in the hospital.

She then asked them how things were going. JR, the oldest, let her know that everything was going okay, that they had everything under control.

"You just focus on getting pops home safe, we will take care of problems in the streets. You should not even be concerned about the streets. You know pops doesn't want you anywhere around the streets," said JR, with a boss like voice.

"Yeah, you just handle pops, we will keep you in the loop, but we have fingers out looking and we will find them, bet that," Devon added.

"Yeah, Mom's, we are men now and can handle ourselves, so you just take care of home, and leave the streets to us", Bobby added.

"Um, I see yaw grown and think you don't need my help. Well let me tell all of you, I was with your father through it all, the good the bad and the ugly. I will be there until hell freezes over. I realize you are all grown, but I'm the Queen. I call the shots with Nickels laid up and don't you forget it.

Now tell me, what the hell is going on out there, and what have you been able to find out," asked Nina, in a voice the three of them had never heard before. She was the Queen and she let them know her voice was the one that mattered.

"The word on the streets is a new gang moved on Luke in San Jose and took over. They have already laid down a few of Luke's men and taken most of his traps. From what we are hearing there are about five or six of them. The leader is a dude named Oscar; people say he came from Houston. He even moved in on Luke's connection with the help of some of Luke's people", replied JR, to Nina.

"Word is that this Oscar dude wants to move weight. He has a crew and they don't seem to care about putting in work", said Devon, to the group.

"Me and Bobby are going to check out the place, a crackhead told Ace, they may be dealing out of, and may be the main bank, so she said. We are going to see what we can find out, and if she is right," said JR.

"Okay... okay... have you ran this by your uncle yet?", asked Nina, while looking around at each of them for a reply.

"No, we have not been able to reach him, I understand that he is running down a dude from the city," replied Devon, from the sofa.

"Yeah, V told me that he left with Roland and Charles going to meet with Frank Dukes from West Oakland", said JR, adding to Devon's comment.

"Frank is the one he took with him to San Jose, looking for the two who shot you and pops," Bobby stated.

"Did you try his pager?" Nina asked.

"Yeah, I tried to page him, but he didn't call back", said JR, looking Nina's way as she walked behind the sofa.

"Well that doesn't mean anything, he doesn't always answer, unless it's Nicholas. Give him a minute and I'm sure he will reach out to you. Meantime, go ahead and check out the house in San Jose and get back at me.

I may be bringing your father home in the morning. Tell Benny and little man that I want them here at seven in the morning", said Nina, and started to walk towards the kitchen. With the conversation drawing to an end, she gave each of them a hug and told them to be careful.

"This is not a game, it is not like the games your father and old John played with you out at the ranch", said Nina, as they walked to the door to leave.

"Don't worry mom, we know it's not a game. Like pop always says, the streets are real and only a fool plays games," they all replied.

***

Nina woke to the sound of the phone ringing. She turned over and picked up the phone on the third ring.

"Hello", said Nina, through a sleepy voice.

"Hey, sleepy head," came the voice.

"Hey, yourself," she responded and smiled.

"Nickels, why are you calling... this early in the morning... Is there something wrong?" Nina said, as she glanced at her clock on the nightstand, seeing it was just past five in the morning.

"No, nothing is wrong, I was thinking about you and wanted to hear your voice," Nickels said.

"I always love to hear your voice, and I'm so glad you feel better. I prayed for you and for God to watch over you,"

Nicholas II A Storm is Coming

"Doc... just left and said I can be released in a couple of hours", said Nicholas, with a great deal of happiness in his voice.

"That's good news, I'll have everything ready here for you", replied Nina, with the same type of joy.

"You need to rest and not worry about anything. Tyrone, the boys and me have everything under control", she stated.

"I know, but I have to make a statement, and I have to find the ones responsible for all of this."

"There will be plenty of time to find out who is behind this when you rest and heal. So, stop worrying about all of that and rest, stop trying to be Mr. Big Shot and let the rest of us help. You need to just hang in the cut and heal."

"Enough about me, how are you doing, is your neck still hurting?" said Nicholas, trying to change the subject.

"I'm doing fine, my neck seems to be healing okay. I still have some pain when I turn my head real sharp. Doctor Logan said I need to wear that damn heavy neck brace for another week, and I should be fine. My arm is doing fine, I just can't move it as fast as I used to", replied Nina, happy to hear Nicholas' voice.

"Well baby, I'm sorry your home coming was so full of drama and all."

"Don't you worry about my home coming, you just get well and come home to me."

"I'm working on that; I want you to call Tyrone and have him bring me some clothes. I want to get out of here now", said Nicholas, while it was getting hard to talk because his throat was hurting, and his jaw was wired. He was trying to talk without moving his jawbone.

"For once, can you just do what the doctor and others tell you? Just rest and wait in the cut, we are handling everything. I will call Tyrone, but he is going to tell you the same thing, rest."

"I'll talk to you later okay...love you", said Nick, and hung up the phone.

Nicholas looked at the phone and thought, *"Thanks for letting me find a good woman."* As he laid back and looked out the window, he couldn't let it go, his mind wanted to know the million-dollar question. Who was it that crossed that line and started this war?

A war that he had hoped would never come, but now the winds were blowing his way and a Storm was Coming. If he were to ever get out the street's and the game, he was going to have to take everybody down that had any part in this action.

The pressing question in his mind was how he was going to handle it. It was going to take a minute for his body to completely heal, yet he had to find them. He was fully determined to find each one of them, believe that.

Getting the cane and the walker that the night nurse left next to his bed, he managed to get up and walk slowly to the bathroom to handle his business.

***

Chapter 37

Juanita was laying on the bed in the nude. She was happy for a few days off. Flip had taken her to the horse track to watch the races. Flip liked the races and he loved to bet on them. He had a good day and had picked three winners. After the track they went to dinner at the pier.

Now in their apartment they both laid on the bed, talking about how best to handle Nicholas. Flip wanted to get the job done and get back to Houston, but Juanita kept telling him about how she was never alone in the room with Nicholas, without a guard standing there watching her every move.

Flip turned her on to her stomach and straddled her back. He started to massage her shoulders rubbing oil on them. She relaxed and allowed herself to enjoy his hands. Flip, moving his hands down her back, as he slid down over her but and spread her legs a little, as he rubbed oil on each of them. He took some warm oil and massaged her legs and upper thighs, working his way down to her feet.

By the time he got to her feet, he was standing on the floor with his dick hard as a rock. Holding her legs open, as he turned her over again on her back, and started to massage her lower inner thighs and the edge of her honey box.

He moved to her breast, as he climbed between her legs, as she arched her back to meet his body. He begins to lick the inner part of her thighs and then his tongue licked the lips of her honey box. While his hand rubbed her nipples, he licked her opening to the point it spread wider and her juices flowed uncontrollably.

He continued making love to her until she couldn't take it any longer and let a built-up orgasm explode from deep within. Her eyes rolled up in her head, as wave after wave of pleasure flowed through her body.

Flip continued to enjoy each time her body would tweak from the pleasure. He positioned himself between her legs, slowly penetrating her honey pot until he had fully submerged his eleven inches deep in her. Gently pulling it out until only the head was in her and then plunged back in her fully. He continued to pump in and out of her, beating up her box, then with one deep push he released his seed deep inside of her.

Juanita could not remember the last time she had been fucked so good or when a man made her feel such passion or have orgasm after orgasm. He continued his pumping manner as he pumped harder and harder. His seed started to flow out of her, squirming out between her lips, running down the crack of her ass to the sheets, Flip continued fucking until he fell over totally exhausted. He just laid between her legs as he went limp inside of her. After laying there for about 10 minutes, she slid out from under him, went into the bathroom, got a hot towel, came back and started to wash him.

She washed her juice and his seed off and started to massage his massive manhood. Looking at the big mushroomed head of his dick, she lowered her head, opened her mouth, and took him in and began to slowly suck and lick his shaft. She sucked his dick until his toes curled and his ass cheeks tightened, and he exploded in her mouth sending his seed down her throat; she swallowed every drop.

They continued making love a third round before falling off to sleep. Juanita got up the next morning and showered, preparing to go to the hospital. She never felt as wanted and loved as she did at that very moment. Flip had taken her heart and soul. She didn't want to lose him and was willing to do anything to please him.

***

Juanita had been off for three days. She didn't know that Nicholas had awaken from his coma and was able to move around with the help of a walker and cane.

She walked past the two guards at the door and entered Nicholas' room. As always, one of the guards stood up and walked behind her into the room and stood by the door. She was shocked to see Nicholas was up and walking out of the bathroom. At first, she just stood there in total disbelief and stared at him.

"Mr. Simmons, what are you doing....I mean when did you wake up... I mean...let me help you?"

"I woke up the other night", Nicholas managed to say, as he made his way back to his bed.

Juanita regained her composure and helped him get in the bed. She was somewhat nervous. She needed to get hold of Flip and find out what to do now. She helped him get comfortable in the bed, then left the room going directly to the nurses station. She picked up the phone and called Flip at the apartment they shared together.

"Flip, Nicholas is woke... yeah he woke up sometime yesterday or the night before, when I was off. I found him walking this morning when I got here, I just came out of his room."

"What do you mean he's woke... Is he fully conscious... does he know where he's at ?"

"Yeah, he seems to be, he's able to move about."

"Are the guards still in the room with you? Is there any chance you can get in there by yourself?

"No, the guard still stands in the room, while I'm there".

"Well, remember what we talked about last night. Can you give him a shot today?"

"I can try since he still has an IV in his arm. I can give him a shot, then leave the building."

"Do that, I'll meet you here at the apartment, how long you think it'll take you?"

"Well, I can go to the pharmacy and get the stuff I need right away. It could take me an hour to get there".

"OK, I'll be here, but hurry, Joseph has located Oscar. I'm going with him to check it out myself... I'll be back within an hour... so, I'll see you then."

"Okay, I'll see you in an hour," Juanita ended the call.

Juanita left the nurses' station, walked to the other wing of the floor to the pharmacy. The pharmacist was not there, but she knew her way around. She was able to get a vile of cyanide and one of morphine. She took both and went back to her station, got a syringe and fixed a lethal shot of cyanide and morphine.

She placed the syringe on a silver tray, took the tray, and started to Nicholas' room.

"Mr. Simmons, I'm going to give you the med's the doctor ordered", said Juanita, in a calm like voice, as she entered Nicholas room.

Nicholas was somewhat taken back by her statement because Doctor Logan had told him that he was not going to order anymore meds, because he would be going home. Doctor Logan had also told him, he was discharging him when they finished his paperwork for him to sign.

"Hold on baby, the nurse just walked in", said Nicholas, looking at her with a great deal of suspicion, wondering why she would be coming in with a syringe.

Nicholas survival instincts took over and set off his survival alarm. Nicholas went to full beast mode; He grabbed her arm before she could administer the medicine in his IV. The guard standing by the door rushed to grab her, the one outside his door rushed in with his gun in his hand. The guard had already grabbed Juanita, holding her as she struggled to get away.

"What the hell's going on," Nina yelled into the phone. "Nick! Nick!", she yelled, and listened for any sound.

"This crazy ass nurse just tried to give me a shot of some kind", said Nick, into the phone.

"Let me call you back in a minute", said Nick, and hung up the phone.

"What are you doing... let me go. I was only doing what the doctor's orders told me", said Juanita, nervously responding, while trying to get away from the guard holding her. "I'm a nurse fool, let me go" she said.

***

154

Hold on to her until we check out her story," Nick told the guard, rising up off the bed. Nicholas sat on the stool next to the bed and pulled the IV needle out of his arm. Nick looked at Juanita with unsympathetic eyes, and the cold stare of a killer.

"Go get my doctor, he should be somewhere in the hospital, maybe in the administration or admittance office, and bring him back here. Oh yeah, don't ask him anything, just bring him."

One of the guards left, headed to the administration office, while shutting the door on the way out. The other guard sat her in the chair and tied her hands with the tubing from the IV and her feet with the cloth belt from a robe.

Using the cane, Nick walked towards her and leaned on the arm of the chair next to her. He looked down at her and asked. "Do you want to change your story and tell me who sent you, and who you work for? I promise it will be better for you to come clean now, than for me to have to make you talk."

"I'm telling you I have done nothing," said Juanita, through tearful eyes. She wasn't scared, she was mad that she got caught. In her mind, she now wondered what was going to happen. She realized she had fucked up and was going to have to pay. Just as she was getting up the nerve to tell a lie, Dr. Logan walked in.

"What's going on in here," he said, surprised to see the nurse in the chair and Nick standing beside the bed.

"Did you tell this nurse to give me a shot?" asked Nick, to Dr. Logan, as he entered the room.

"No! I did not tell her anything, I had not even seen her today. I told you before I went to get your paperwork, you will not need anything until you get home and fill the prescription."

"Thank you, doc, now let us have this room."

The doctor turned, looked at the young woman in the chair and thought that it was best he forgot he knew her. He left the room and went to the nurse's station.

He sat down at the desk putting his hands over his eyes and tried to think. "What could he possibly do in order to get the nurse out of the bad situation she had gotten herself in?" Coming up with nothing that seemed to make any since, he got up and left the hospital.

Nick stood there looking at the nurse, showing no emotion or remorse." Who sent you?"

"I don't know what you are talking about", replied Juanita, trying to act innocent, yet, extremely nervous.

"Boss, I paged Tyrone, but I didn't get him", said one of the guards.

Juanita continued to cry, as she looked at the two guards standing over her. One of the guards started to screw a long silencer on the end of his gun. Looking at the gun and then at Nick, she let out a long sigh, then broke down.

Nicholas stood there looking at her with a considerable amount of animosity in his eyes. Nick wanted to shoot her, but he needed to know who was behind the hit. They sat there for about twenty minutes before Tyrone walked in. Tyrone looked like the devil himself to her.

"Has she talked yet," Tyrone asked.

"Yes and No... She claims she is a nurse, and works for the agency", said Nick.

"Well, we will see what she says when she gets out to the ranch", said Tyrone, in a cold-hearted manner.

"Take her to the car and make sure she is tied tight. Put something over her head and tape her mouth so she can't talk", instructed Tyrone, to the guards.

"What about the hospital people and Dr. Logan, they will see us taking her, won't they have questions if she comes up missing?", the guard asked.

Nicholas II A Storm is Coming

"Right now, let's not worry about Dr. Logan, we can handle him later, but get her out of here before anybody else sees her," Tyrone said, while looking at the nurse's desk and workstation.

***

It was still early; the day shift had not come on yet and had not made it to the floor. By walking her down the back stairwell, they avoided the staff coming off the elevator for their shift. They got Juanita out the hospital and into Tyrone's town car without anyone noticing.

Nicholas picked up the phone and called Nina, but no one answered. Because when he hung up before, she had gotten up, dressed, and was headed to the hospital. Nicholas hung the phone up just as Nina came around the corner from the hallway into his room.

She noticed the day shift nursing staff was just getting in. She also noticed that the private nurse, the brunette was not at her station. There were only two other people on the floor with Nicholas and both were old and in private rooms with the doors shut, therefore, they could not have heard or seen anything.

"Nick, is everything okay... Why did you hang up on me...what's going on?" said Nina, while running into Nick's arms, causing him to fall back on the bed. Nicholas was still weak and needed to sit down. His mouth was sore, and he could not really talk, because of the wire holding his jaw shut.

The doctor had said Nick didn't need any pain medicines before this incident but believe it, right now he could use a pill or shot of something, his jaw was killing him, and he could do nothing.

"It's okay now baby, I had to handle a little problem with the nurse, but it's all been taken care of now."

"Was it that brunette who works day shift?"

"Yeah, she tried to give me a shot of something, however, I have taken care of it; she's on the way to the ranch."

"Is the bitch dead? Please tell me she is not, so I can put my foot in her ass and then kill her myself."

157

"No, she is not dead, I need to get some information from her, like who is behind all of this. Someone paid her to do it and I need to find him or them", said Nick, with a great deal of pain.

"You... stop talking and lie down and rest, I will handle things from here", said Nina, and tried to help Nick get back in the bed.

"No, I want to get up out of here now, did you leave any clothes here for me? I want to get home and then we can handle our business."

"Yes, I left a pair of slacks and a shirt and shoes in the cabinet for you. I'll get them."

She got the clothes, and Nick got dressed and called the guard. "Get a wheelchair and roll me out of here. Your car, is it downstairs in the front or back?" Nicholas asked Nina.

"It is in the front parking lot. I'll get it and bring it to the front door. You watch after him," she told the guard, and hurried to the elevator.

Nicholas got in Nina's Car and told the guard to stay one car behind them. "Hey, what kind of car do you have?", asked Nicholas.

"A blue mercury," he replied.

Nickolas sat there and looked around to make sure that no one was watching. He told Nina to be sure that no one was following and to double back over the bridge to Oakland, and double back to the house, so they could check for any cars following them.

***

Opening the trunk of the car Tyrone took a scared Juanita out, then led her into the shed. He tied her to the chair and started asking her questions. He soon found that she didn't rattle easy, she had been through interrogation and torture treatments while in custody in Mexico. So, frightening her, was not getting him any answers.

Tyrone soon realized slapping her around or pouring water down her mouth was not gonna break her. He took a pair of pliers and pulled the finger nail from her baby finger. Blood squirted out her finger, and she screamed from the pain. He continued to pull her fingernails out, one at a time, causing a great deal of pain. She hollered and screamed, but refused to answer his questions.

When he grabbed her head and pried her mouth open, he applied the pliers to a tooth, she looked at him. Not with a look of sorrow, but one of hate. He thought she was about to break. As he started to pull her teeth out, one by one, blood began to run down her throat, she screamed, "OK...OK... I'll tell you... I'll tell you."

"Now, are you ready to tell me the truth", said Tyrone, with a look of I can go on if not.

Juanita told him a big fat set of lies, that she thought would protect Flip, but Tyrone didn't believe her.

After a couple of hours of telling the same lie over and over he realized she was not going to change her story. She was willing to die rather than give up her man. Old school to the end. Tyrone had to respect her gangster and left her hands tied, but removed her from the chair, placed her in a little cell, crying and in great pain.

***

Nicholas was resting after getting home from the hospital. Nina came into the room, picked up the phone, and handed it to him.

"Here, it's Danny, he wants to say hi", said Nina, handing him the phone, with a look of apprehension on her face.

"Hello, my friend", said Nick, sitting up in the bed trying to talk through a wired jaw.

"Hello to you too my friend, don't try to talk just listen," came the reply. Nick could tell from the sound of his voice that Danny had something on his mind.

"How are you feeling?"

"I have been better", replied Nick.

"Well, my friend, you just take it easy and get well, Nina has told me what happened, and I will get to the bottom of it," he said, with a great deal of concern in his voice.

"Thank you, but I will handle it", Nick managed to say.

"Now Nick, you are not in any shape to be running around getting any answers. I can send some people to help find the one who did this my friend," Danny said.

"No, I don't want any more strangers in my town. I will find them, and deal with it, you understand? Thank you for your concerns, but this is my trouble not yours", said Nick, straining to talk and bearing the pain from trying.

Nick handed the phone back to Nina and waved his hands for her to talk to Danny for him.

"Danny, this is Nina, what my husband is trying to say is that he has to take care of this, if he wants to continue to run the WCC (West Coast Cartel). If you do it, then you are the one who the streets will fear. He must handle it, so the other dealers and the streets know he is the boss, so that no one will dare step to him like this again. You understand?"

"Si, I understand and I'm here if you need me. I will leave it up to you. Let me know if you need anything", he replied, and then hung up the phone.

Nicholas II A Storm is Coming

Nina placed the phone back on the nightstand and looked at Nick. He was in a great deal of pain from trying to talk. She got him a glass of water and handed him a pain pill. Nick took the pill, laid back on the pillow, and tried to get some rest.

***

Nick was having a hell of a time because his mind was working overtime trying to figure out who was behind the hit. Nick knew Tyrone was going to have to get the nurse to talk and tell who hired her.

Nick just couldn't figure out how they knew he was going to be at the airport.

Nina laid down next to him and placed his head on her breast and rubbed it while saying, "just lay back and get well, everything is going to work out; you have to get your strength up before you get out there looking for the one who did this."

Nick laid there and let the pill do its job, it put him on easy street, and he fell off into a semi- deep sleep.

The next morning, he woke to the smell of coffee and turned in the bed to find Nina had poured him a cup of coffee and brought the paper. Nick sat up in the bed and tried to drink a little coffee while she handed him a glass of orange juice to take his pills. He sat there, drank the coffee and read the paper. "Have you talked to Tyrone this morning," Nick asked her, when she walked back in the room.

"No, I haven't talked to him, but I did talk to V. She said he was out at the ranch most of the night."

Nick replied, "Oh yeah, that was a sure sign that someone had been undergoing questioning Tyrone style, you know how he likes the beat down, and if he had blood on himself, he would take a shower before leaving the ranch and going home," said Nick, while looking at the stock exchange index in the paper.

"Try to reach him for me and tell him I need to talk to him", said Nick, as he finished the coffee and put the paper down.

Tyrone arrived at the house and walked into the bedroom. He started to tell Nick about the nurse.

"That little bitch claims she doesn't know anything. She claims she got the call from a man, but doesn't know him, claims she never met him. She said he first called her and told her he wanted her to be a nurse for a friend. She said he would deposit a thousand each week into her bank account. I believe she is lying and there is more to it than she is telling. She is a hard cookie and she has done time before; I can tell by the way she takes pain. But she will break in time, they all do, it's just a matter of time. He also wanted to know how many guards you had, and any information she could give him on your condition.

She was told to call a number to report on your condition. She was told not to tell or let anyone know. I checked her bank account... she did get a wire deposit of one thousand a week for the past four weeks. However, there is no record of who made the deposit. They were wired from a bank in the Cayman Islands, from a Cayman bank numbered account."

***

I also took care of that little white dude, William Franklin and his bitch."

"Wait, what the hell you doing with William Franklin? He's just a little punk ass white boy, who wants to be a pimp."

"Yeah, we picked him and his bitch up at the Cattlemen's two weeks back. Turns out William was the driver of the van. He also handled the money and paid the two Mexican hitter's Oscar and Juan, two Mexicans from Houston. He also paid two small time hustler's from Oakland to finger you. A nigga named P-Slim and his partner Dirty Mike.

Those two followed you around and then told Williams you were going to the airport. I have not got my hands on them yet. But I have word on where I can find them," said Tyrone, with a concern look on his face.

Nicholas II A Storm is Coming

"No way, you couldn't have told me William had balls big enough to handle a hit. Goes to show you never know the way the streets are changing", replied Nicholas, while shaking his head.

"They are changing, and not for the best", added Tyrone, while updating Nicholas on the hunt for the boss who ordered the hit.

"I bet Old John must be having fits with all the people coming and going out there," said Nicholas, as they walked toward the kitchen.

***

N ow the word on the streets was P-Slim had gotten locked up. He was being held in Greystone awaiting his trial. He was talking shit about how he was going to beat the case and then leave town.

Tyrone was outraged when they told him they were not able to get at him under normal means. Tyrone wanted to bail him out himself, but the judge had put P-Slim under a no bail hold, so that idea would not fly. Tyrone called a captain in the Sheriff's Department on the take to feel him out about using someone on the inside to get at P-Slim. However, the captain told Tyrone that he had been transferred from Santa Rita four months back, so he was of no help.

Tyrone thought to himself "that sucker was safe for the moment. He would have to come up with some other way to get his hands-on P-Slim."

***

Dirty Mike's car was found parked on the back streets by the bus station. Word was he may have been robbed and killed, since blood was found in the car. The fact was Dirty Mike had taken a Greyhound out of town.

The question was where he went. After two weeks of asking questions an old crackhead came to a trap house on 28th and Market. He told the dealer who ran the house, "give me five rocks and I'll tell you where Dirty Mike is", said the old crackhead, rubbing his hands and smelling like shit. Ricky, the guy who dealt out of the trap gave him two rocks. The old crackhead told him he saw Dirty Mike get on the nine-thirty bus a couple of weeks back. Ricky called Tyrone with the news and Tyrone checked it out.

Tyrone got with Ricky and they checked where the bus at nine-thirty went. They found that there was only one bus that departed between nine-thirty and ten o' clock. That bus was headed to Bakersfield, so with that information, Tyrone sent Charles and Ace to Bakersfield to see if they could find Dirty-Mike.

***

Flip, after talking to Juanita, got up and handled his business in the bathroom. He got dressed and called Joseph, his main man, to pick him up. They were going to an area of San Jose. He hoped to find Oscar and take him out the picture so he and Juanita could get back to Houston when she finished Nicholas.

It was showing signs of rain as he and joseph got in the car. He was thinking that if he could catch Oscar at the trap house, he could hit him and be back at the apartment within an hour.

Little did he know that Juanita had taken one for him and was in Tyrone's hands. Joseph was having a hard time seeing the road as the rain was heavy, and the streets wet and slippery. It was a couple of weeks before Thanksgiving and the biggest storm of the year was passing through the bay area.

***

Joseph found his way to the location he believed Oscar was dealing from, and he parked a half block away.

The rain was so heavy, they could not see the house good, but it was clear that it was a trap house. While they sat there, several crackheads had gone in and out of the house. Flip was hoping to see Oscar, but he didn't see anyone come out the house that looked like him.

He sat in the car and tried to think of a way to get Oscar to come out of the house. Coming up with no idea that made any sense, he was lost for a minute. Then he thought about the fact that Oscar didn't know Joseph. He could have Joseph go in and make a buy. He could get Oscar to come outside, where he could shoot him and leave.

After running the plan down to Joseph, who was okay with the idea, Joseph got out the car in the rain and headed to the trap house. He made it to the door and disappeared in the house. After about five

A B Hudson

minutes, he walked out with Oscar right behind him. Joseph walked down the steps and headed toward the little fenced gate.

I pulled the car in gear and started to drive toward the house. As I got in front of the house Joseph pulled his gun and turned and fired at Oscar. Joseph fired three rounds and started to run toward the car. Oscar ducked, as he saw the car pull up, and started reaching for his 45 under his shirt. Oscar got two shots off before two of the bullets that Joseph fired hit Oscar. One in the chest and one in his left arm, the third one missed his head. Wounded, Oscar made it back to the porch and ducked behind the rail. Flip and Joseph pulled out in the street and Flip gunned the engine and headed up the street.

"We got him", said Joseph, as he fell into the passenger seat. He didn't realize at the time that he had taken one in his lower back. His adrenaline was flowing so fast. However, now starting to feel a sharp pain in his lower back as the nerves started to come back to life, he yelled, "I'm hit." Flip pulled over to the side of the road to look at him.

Back at the house Oscar was laying on the porch bleeding, Jackie was crying in the phone with the 911 operator.

"Please send an ambulance, my man has been shot", said Jackie, to the operator.

"Miss, please tell me the address where you are", replied the operator.

Giving her the address, Jackie kept telling Oscar, "Hold on baby, help is on the way."

"Get the house clean," said Oscar, while dealing with the pain in his chest.

By the time the ambulance and police got there Jackie and Poncho had hid the drugs and money. She put the money and drugs in her car out back.

The police looked at Oscar and called for backup to check the house. They knew it was going to be clean, as it took them almost thirty minutes to get there. The police were good at missing a shooting, until

166

they felt the shooting was over, then they would come in and pick up the remains.

They removed Oscar from the porch and took him to the hospital. He had lost a lot of blood but was still alive. When the paramedics got him to the hospital, he was still alive going into the operating room.

***

Chapter 40

Monday morning Nicholas had a Dentist appointment. He was going to the dentist to have the last three implants put in his left jaw and to have the wire removed. He was still having pain in the jaw but was able to handle it. His face had healed but his skin was still tight and felt funny. He could not shave due to the work the plastic surgeon had did. Doctor Tillman had told him it could be up to two years before hair would grow on his face again.

When he got dressed and made it to the kitchen, Nina was sitting there drinking a cup of coffee, while Mrs. Green was going on about her new pastor and how he was preaching about the streets.

He walked over to Nina and told her, "good morning", and placed a kiss on her forehead and then said, "hello", to Mrs. Green.

"Hello Mr. Simmons... Good morning to you, would you like coffee?", replied Mrs. Green, with a smile.

"Yes, I could use a cup... thank you", said Nick, while smiling back at her.

Taking the cup and grabbing a hot bun he headed to his den. He picked up the phone and called Tyrone. "Hello V let me talk to your old man," said Nicholas when Vivian answered the phone.

"Hey, hello Nick, just a minute, he is outside," she said, and placed the phone on the counter.

"Hey... baby, its Nick on the phone", Nick could hear her yell.

After a moment, "Hey Nick what up?", said Tyrone, sounding like he was out of breath.

"Oh, nothing too much, same old shit, just a new day", said Nick.

"Look, I need to go to the dentist, and I wanted to talk over some things with you, can you pick me up in an hour?", asked Nick.

"I'll will be there in an hour. Did Mrs. Green cook?", asked Tyrone.

"Yeah, she cooked, why... you want me to have her save something for you?"

"Hell yeah... you know that woman can burn."

"Okay, I'll tell her, and I'll see you in a minute", said Nick, as he ended the conversation. He sat back in his chair and ate the honey bun and finished his coffee, while reading the paper.

***

Flip made it back to the apartment, only to find that Juanita was not there. He tried to call the hospital, but the nurse that answered said that she had not seen her, she didn't come in to work.

He knew from her statement that something was wrong. He could only guess that she got caught and that she might tell where he was. He got Joseph up off the sofa and helped him back to the car. Joseph had gotten hit in the side in the shootout. Now Flip needed to get somewhere safe and regroup. He had to find out what happen to Juanita. He needed to know if she gave Nicholas the shot.

Joseph was still bleeding, but not as bad as before, he was able to walk with help. So, they made it to the car and were headed to the hospital to get him some help.

Flip took him in the emergency room and told the nurse that he was shot by someone trying to rob him. It worked for the moment, Flip knew Joseph would get some help, so he left him and went looking to find Juanita.

When he got back to the apartment, he drove around the block a couple of times to be sure no one was watching him. He went in and got all of his stuff and left again. He went to the airport and saw that he could get a flight out to Dallas if he left right then. So, he decided he had to leave her and get out while he could. He had to think she had gotten caught or was killed.

Oscar had made it through the surgery. He was in the ICU guarded by the police. Jackie had gone to the Mountain Valley Hospital to check on Oscar. Once she found that he was in ICU guarded by the police, she left. Jackie and Poncho were staying at a motel hiding from Flip. Believing Flip was looking for them, as well as Oscar. She didn't know if Oscar had shot Flip in the shootout, but she was taking no chances. She was going to wait until she could see Oscar and figure out what to do next.

The police wanted to question Oscar about the shooting, so they placed a hold on him at the hospital. They knew he was Involved in some way, they just didn't know how, or if he was a boss or worker, or just a crackhead trying to buy a rock.

Over the past month and a half, they had picked up on the word that a new gang had moved in on the local boys. The police had responded to five shootings in two weeks. So, they knew this one was no different. They just wanted to keep the shooting and killing on the east side and away from the so-called decent folks.

***

Tyrone drove to Nick's while thinking, *"it had been over two months and they had not found who ordered the hit. He had already killed five or six people, yet he was no closer to an answer of who. He was still looking for this guy named Flip, and someone named Oscar, and a guy named Juan, who were the one's believed to be the shooters."* Tyrone started to go over all the clues he had as he continued to Nick's house.

Tyrone pulled into the driveway; he saw the gardener riding a lawn mower. He thought about the fact that he needed to cut his own grass. Parking and walking to the front door, he rang the door bell, Mrs. Green opened the door and said, "come in... how have you been Mr. Tyrone...How is Miss Vivian...when are you two going to make the jump", said Mrs. Green, as she was like a mother hen to all of them. Tyrone walked past her and said, "I'm fine and Vivian is doing fine. I'm surprised you are not in on the planning of the wedding, that I'm not supposed to know about," replied Tyrone, letting her know that he was on to their little plan. Then he changed the subject, "Did you cook any of those biscuits and bacon this morning?"

"Boy... you a mess... you know I cook biscuits every morning, don't try to sweet talk me. I'm hip to you...go in the kitchen and I will get you something to eat."

They walked into the kitchen, to find Nina sitting at the counter with a cup of coffee, while she was looking at flight schedules for her parents and brother to fly out for Thanksgiving.

"Hey baby girl, what's happening with you this morning?", asked Tyrone, as he took a piece of bacon from the tray on the counter.

"Hey yourself, big head, I was just going over some flight schedules. I'm planning a dinner for Thanksgiving", replied Nina, as she continued to drink her coffee.

"Stop putting your big mitts in my tray... sit down at the table and I will fix you a plate," snapped Mrs. Green.

Just as Mrs. Green started to fix his plate, Nick walked in the kitchen. "I thought I heard you in here," he said with a smile.

"Hey Nick, how's it going?", said Tyrone, while chewing on a biscuit with bacon.

"Mrs. Green stop feeding that big ape, he is big enough already", said Nick, joking.

"See, you always talking about somebody, but when I talk about your ass you want to get mad. Just leave me alone and let me enjoy my biscuit", said Tyrone, without stopping his chewing. He finished his biscuit and grabbed one to go.

Mrs. Green just smiled and thought to herself, *"that man looks and acts just like my late husband, God rest his soul."* She snapped out of her thoughts and started to clear the counter and table. She had gotten the job to cook for Nina when Nina had been shot. She could not be happier with the job.

Her last job was for an old white woman who she didn't like very much but worked for because she needed the job. However, when Vivian hired her to cook for Nina, she was only supposed to cook for two or three weeks. Nina made her feel so at home that she quit the other woman and started working full time for Nina, not to mention the substantial increase in pay. She was now able to send her granddaughter, a couple of dollars every month, to help with her two great grandkids.

***

Nicholas and Tyrone walked into Nick's den, Tyrone started to update him on what had been happening and where he was with the hunt for the one behind the shooting. He also gave Nick an update on how the products and money was going.

They talked about the crew and how they were going to handle the product. Tyrone told him how Frank was handling his business, and how far he had come. He talked about how John was running the projects and house's in Vallejo. He also told Nick about the new gang that was in San Jose. He was still mad about the boy's going to San Jose the other day but didn't show it.

Nick said, "Let's talk on the way, I have to get to this dentist appointment," he said, and started to put on his coat.

Tyrone looked at his watch and said, "yeah we got time, your appointment is at eleven and it's only ten-fifteen."

Nick looked at him like you know I like to be on time. With that they got up and headed to the car.

***

They continued to talk as he drove to the dentist. Nicholas sat there, listening, looking out the window. "I was thinking that whoever ordered the hit had to be someone with a lot of information on me," Nicholas stated, and looked at Tyrone as he drove.

Nicholas continued to think to himself. Trying to come up with names of people who had the balls to order a hit at an airport of all places. *"William didn't fit the bill or have the balls to hurt an ant on the table, let alone order a hit. He was a foolish man but not a killer."*

No, the person Nick was looking for had big balls and a reason to come at him. Nick was still in his thoughts, when Tyrone said, "Nick, are you sleep or something, we are here, let's get out the car," said Tyrone, while touching Nick's arm.

"Okay, I just dozed off for a moment thinking about who could be behind this mess," Nick replied, as they got out the car.

***

"Good morning, please sign in and have a seat, Doctor Bondsman will see you in a few minutes," the nurse said through the window. Tyrone and Nicholas took a seat and waited for the nurse to call his name.

"Nick, let me ask, what you think was the reason for the hit in the first place", asked Tyrone, with a puzzled expression.

"Well, I have been thinking about that, and I can't come up with any one reason", replied Nicholas, giving him the same puzzled look.

"Do you think it has anything to do with Danny and Jimmy? I'm just saying that because we don't deal with the street directly. So, I don't see any street dealers coming at you like that, said Tyrone, as they continued to talk between themselves.

"I have not ruled it out, I talked to Danny and he wanted me to let Carlos from El Paso come up and help. But I shut that down, I let him know that I would find out and handle this mess myself. So, we need to be on point, until we find out who ordered it and handle them. We have to keep our heads in the game."

***

"Nicholas Simmons", the nurse said, from the door that led to the treatment rooms.

"Yes, that's me", said Nicholas, and got up and walked to the door.

"This way please", said the nurse, and led him to a room. She instructed him to have a seat in the chair and placed a bib around his neck.

"The doctor will be right in", said the nurse, and walked out the room closing the door behind her.

Nicholas was getting the new implants today, and he was anxious to find out how he looked. The plastic surgeon had finished his work rebuilding Nicholas jawbone, and the left side of his face. Nicholas was still hurting from all the skin graphs and work on his jaw to line it up right. Nicholas guessed he should be happy he was able to have the work done, a few centimeters higher and he would not be here.

Nicholas got caught slipping and almost lost his life, and the love of his life, Nina. She was doing well but had developed a phobia about cars coming up next to them or her when driving. Nicholas guessed getting shot could do that to a person. Hopefully, she would get over it in time.

The dentist came in and started working. After an hour and a half, he was telling his assistant to wash the blood out of Nicholas' mouth, and to remove the suction tool that hung in the corner of his mouth; Nicholas was still half-sleep and half-awake from the meds.

After Nicholas was fully awake and was getting used to the feeling of the implants the dentist walked in, "How do we feel Mr. Simmons?", he asked.

"Man, Doc, I feel okay I guess, but my mouth feels funny", Nicholas said.

The new teeth did not feel too bad, not as bad as he thought they would, and they were better than having none.

Nicholas walked out of the treatment room. Tyrone was sitting there looking at the newspaper while checking the nurse behind the counter. He was not looking at her as if he were going to do anything, but what in the hell did she have on her head.

The color of the nurse's hair was blue, green, and orange, and she had a tear drop on the side of her face and a spider web on her neck. She was dressed in all black and dark circles around her eyes. Tyrone was looking at her like, what was her problem?

As Nicholas walked over to the chair where Tyrone was sitting, he got up, looked at Nicholas face, and said, "you have looked better, but I guess it will work. You better be glad you got Nina, because with a mug like yours, only a mother would love you", then Tyrone smiles.

"Fuck you, big head."

"Yeah, you look pretty good for an old man, how do the new teeth feel?"

"They are okay I guess; I have to get used to them."

"I guess that will happen over time, did they take that wire out?

Yeah, but it still hurts to talk".

"Let's get out of here, I want to go to the ranch."

"Are you sure you want to go out there?

"Yeah, I need to get back on the job, I want to get to the bottom of this."

" I hear that, but where do we start...I've been hitting the streets and all, but nothing is coming in. It's like the ones who did this are dug in deep and we have not been able to find the hole, yet. But believe me I will find them.

***

How is John taking to all the people coming and going?", asked Nick, with a smile on his face.

"He is mad as a ho in church", replied Tyrone.

Old John, an ex-panther and army ranger, lived on the ranch and didn't like people around him. He was a loner and had issues with people. He taught Nicholas, Tyrone, and most of the rest of the family how to survive in the wilderness, how to hunt and fish. He taught them how to move without making a sound. How to survive using only the items and tools that they found.

The best had trained him, the U.S. government. They had used him in Vietnam to kill. Then after the Vietnam war ended, they drummed him out of the Rangers, causing him to withdraw from people, taking himself off the grid altogether.

"He drove me back to town the other night, to get my car, and he talked my ear off about shit he had to put up with when he was in the army. Also, about when he came back from Vietnam. He is not a happy camper with all the shit he went through. Did you know he had over three hundred kills in the war?"

"Yeah, back when the party was going strong, he was the one who showed me how to shoot from almost a mile away. He taught me how to hit my target and to get away without anyone knowing that I was even there", said Nicholas, with a spark in his eye.

***

"Now with crack taking hold of the streets, and youngsters standing on corners selling rocks, as if they had a license; it's a different world. Yeah, we were making money, it was a good thing in a way, but bad in other ways. However, I did not make the rules, nor did I tell or make people use drugs. "

"You know the FBI and DEA are starting to put agents in the streets and they are cracking down on the crack dealers," but crack was winning the fight, for every crackhead they locked up three more would take their place. That shit has people coming out the woodwork and climbing over their babies to get to that glass dick and a rock. I remember when coke was just snorted, used to have a good time. Now, they smoke it, they're cooking it, and the streets have gone hog-shit wild," said Tyrone, with a disgusted look on his face.

***

As they drove to the ranch Nicholas sat in the seat and looked out over the land. He was in deep thought about who could be behind the shooting. Now that he was up and getting around fairly good, he was going to get to the bottom of the whole mess.

The nurse was the key to finding the one who was the mastermind. Tyrone had told him that she was not going to break. When they turned off the main road, headed toward the house, Tyrone pointed out the two new gun Tarrats located about seventy-five yards off the main road.

"I see you stepped up the security", said Nick, as he looked around the fields of corn. After turning off the main road, they still had a quarter of a mile to get to the house. When they got to the house, Nick first when over to the little house, and talked to John for a few minutes, before going to the shed.

It took Nicholas a moment to get use to the smell in the shed. Juanita had been tied up for two days and she smelled bad. Besides the beating and blood along with the pain, she had shit and peed on the floor, in the little cell she was in.

Nick walked over to the cell and took her out and sat her on a chair. Her hands were tied, so he just tied her to the chair with a rope around her chest and legs. He then pulled her head up to meet his eyes.

"Remember me... I'm the one you wanted to kill", said Nick, as he looked at her in pure disgust.

She tried to turn her head, but couldn't, tried to talk, but no sound came out her mouth. She was exhausted and hunger was driving her insane. She just wanted the pain to stop, to go ahead and die. She knew she wasn't getting out of this shed. She had been praying that death would take her. She even welcomed death so she could be done. She wasn't gonna give up Flip under no circumstances, she was a ride and die bitch to the end.

***

Nicholas looked around the shed and saw a chair in the corner, he went to get it and brought it back and sat right in front of her. He was now seeing what Tyrone saw in her. She was not going to break, but he had to ask her one last time.

"Tell me who sent you and this will all be over; I promise you I will end it quick. But if you don't tell me, I'll keep giving you pain like you never imagined. Is the one who sent you worth that?", asked Nicholas.

Juanita tried to open her eyes, but they were both black and blue and swollen shut. But the expression she gave him let him know she was not going to talk.

"Okay have it your way," replied Nicholas, in a cold-hearted manner. He stood up and pulled the 9mm from his lower back, aimed it at her head and pulled the trigger two times. Blood and brain matter shot out the back of her head and hit the wall behind the chair.

***

Nicholas put the gun away and walked out the shed and back to the house where
Tyrone and John were talking.

"You were right she was not going to talk," said Nicholas.

"John, get some of the guys to clean that shit up and feed her to the hogs", said Nicholas.

"There are people who will take it to the max, but most will break before they reach that point. She was a hard bitch", said John, with a nod of his head.

"Let's get back to the work at hand. Have you got any ideas who this person could be?", asked Nick, talking to Tyrone and John.

"No, I did find out or should I say the boy's found out that a new gang killed Luke and took over San Jose. JR and Devon have been watching them for a couple of days."

"Do you know who they are, or where they came from?", asked Nick, as he tried to think of anybody he could remember talking about moving in on San Jose.

"No, I hear that the leader is from Houston, but I have not confirmed that", said Tyrone.

"Okay, let's start there, run down what you know about this gang, said Nick.

***

After Tyrone and John gave him an update of all they knew about the new gang, and they downed three beers apiece, it was going on five in the afternoon. Nicholas thought he was good, but was starting to feel sore, and his mouth was starting to hurt a little. He turned to John and said, "I think I better get on home and take something for this pain and get some rest. I will get at you in a day or two," said Nick.

"Yeah, you better get home before Nina gets in that ass", replied Tyrone. John didn't say a word, he just looked at both of them. Nick and Tyrone both got up and headed to the door. John started to remove the beer bottles from the table and clean up; he was going to go fishing after they left.

***

The drive to Nick's house was quick and quiet. As soon as Nick and Tyrone opened the door, Nina started, "Where have you been all day. You were supposed to go to the dentist and come home. Now where have you two been?" Nina fussed as Nick and Tyrone just continued into the living room and sat down.

They both knew better than to talk while she was talking. When she stopped to take a breath, she looked at Nicholas and Tyrone, she

179

threw up both of her hands and said, "you are driving me insane," she replied, and walked out the living room with a don't fuck with me look on her face.

"Pick me up tomorrow about nine, we are going to Richmond, so be prepared," said Nick, as he got up and headed upstairs when he saw Nina turn the corner going to the kitchen. He was going to get something for the pain in his jaw.

"Okay, I'll see you then, will you be okay with that woman tonight?", asked Tyrone, in a joking manner, looking around to see if Nina heard him.

While the two of them were O.G.'s and two of the baddest niggas to walk the street, they both knew Nina was a handful when she got mad. Nick was not alone, Tyrone knew he was in for the same treatment when he got home, from Vivian. She was just as bad as Nina.

***

Nicholas II A Storm is Coming
Chapter 42

The next morning Tyrone picked Nick up at nine. They headed to the warehouse to meet with some of the crew. Nicholas had not been to the warehouse since before the shooting. He was somewhat excited to see everyone. Last night he had called his son's, Nicholas Jr, Devon and Bobby, telling them to be there. He also called John and Frank.

By the time Tyrone and Nick got there everyone was talking and wondering what was going down. Nicholas walked to the table and took his seat. Everyone sat and turned toward him.

"It is nice to see all of your faces", said Nick, in an effortless voice.

Everyone said, "hi", and started speaking at the same time. Nick told them all hi and stated he would chat with each of them later, right now he had some business that needed to be taken care of first.

"I know you are wondering why we are here today. Well the short answer is, I have a meeting today with all the heads of the families in the bay area. We are going to sit down and settle this problem. They are going to tell me who was behind the shooting and hand them over to me. Then we are going to move forward," said Nicholas, with a boldness in his voice.

"How we going to get them to talk and tell us who did it?", replied Bobby, trying to sound like he knew what he was saying.

"We are going to make them an offer, basically let them know, if I don't get the one who masterminded this, I will burn down the rest of them finding him", said Nicholas, with a great deal of attitude in his voice.

"Pop, we have been looking upside down for the mastermind, but there is not anything that leads us to believe anyone here in the bay area was the leader. It's like it was an outside job," said Nick Jr., in a smooth voice.

"Well, that is what I plan to find out today for sure", stated Nicholas.

Everyone just looked at him and thought to themselves, *"What does he have up his sleeve. Nicholas doesn't do anything without thinking about it and planning at least five steps ahead."*

"With all that said, I want you Frank, and John, to follow the Italian's when they leave the meeting, and tell me where they go", said Nicholas, looking at the both of them.

"Okay boss, we are on it", said John and Frank, looking at each other and then at Nicholas.

"JR, I want you to follow the head of the Chinese, he most likely will be with two maybe three bodyguards, follow him; I wanna know where he goes", said Nicholas.

"Devon, I want you to follow the Japanese, like your brother, I don't want you to do anything, just follow him and let me know where he goes."

"Bobby, you're gonna follow the Russian. I have a fairly good idea where he's going, but I want you to keep an eye on him, then report to me."

"Now guys, I want you to be very inconspicuous, and use all the training and teaching John taught you, about how to move without being seen. I need you to use all the skills you know.

Tyrone and me, we're gonna be at the meeting. I suspect that everyone is going to go and report to their own people, if one of them is part of this whole thing, we're gonna find out today. I want everybody to meet back here at 8:00 o'clock tonight." With everyone having instructions and understanding the severity, everyone left.

Frank Dukes and John Robertson knew each other from reputation only. Frank ran most of the lower bottom and a good portion of Richmond and all of Berkeley. While John took his mother Frances' seat, he ran all of Vallejo, Fairfax, Hercules, and Sacramento. Even did a little dealing in Stockton along with the central valley. They were the new King's on the turf, along with Nicholas' sons, Nicholas Jr, Devon, and Bobby. They were the ones who were going to be taking over the game.

When everyone said their goodbyes, they all left Nicholas and Tyrone sitting in the office alone.

"Well it's been awhile since we've had to have a war meeting", said Nicholas.

"Yeah, the last time the mafia came after us, we laid a lot of them down. I must be getting old, this is not as much fun anymore", said Tyrone, flexing his arms and looking at his hands.

"Look, I don't know about you, I'm looking forward to getting out. The bank deal came through", said Nicholas, with a great smile on his face. Tyrone didn't know, he too, was an extraordinarily rich man with legitimate finance.

"That's great, you own a bank now", said Tyrone, with a great deal of pride in his voice.

"Well, we don't own a bank. We control the stock of the bank, we... Nina and I control 58% of the public stock, you own 20%, and the rest of the crew are in for 15%, spread out between them. So that means, all in all we own 93% of all the public stock out there.

Then given the fact that Simmons Enterprise Incorporated is doing very well, Simmons Engineering has five major contracts, over five hundred million each. Looks like we are getting the bid on four water treatment plants and a couple of other big projects in the next few months.

The HNN&T accounting firm has four of the largest corporations in the state. OGFR Realtors is doing a booming business in real estate, commercial and residential. So, I say we are in rather good shape, to be able to step away.

It's time, remember when we first got in this game. We knew the day would come when we would have to step aside. You get laid down or sent to prison for the rest of your life if you hang around too long; I choose to step down on my own. Go off and do my thing. I can't spend all the money I have right now, let the youngsters eat a piece of the pie. They got the energy and hunger to survive the next generation of the streets and the game".

***

The meeting of all the heads was at two in the dining room of Polo's. The Italian mafia, Russian mafia, Chinese, and Filipino leaders were there. Nicholas thanked everybody for coming, sat down and told everyone his intent; to find the person or persons that orchestrated, the attempt to assassinate him.

He was not there to negotiate; he wanted the person or persons who orchestrated it. If he had to go about finding them in his own way, their actions could lead to a lot of innocent people getting caught in crossfire. Which also meant if he had to come into their turf, he was going to cross that line. He didn't really care because he wasn't gonna live in fear of them coming after him again.

His rule was never let anyone who wanted to do you harm, get away, and have a second chance to come at you if they missed the first time. "So, gentlemen, the choice is up to you, help me, or get out of my way", said Nicholas, as he looked around the room.

All the leaders of the respected organizations sat there listening at and looking at Nicholas. They fully understood the potential cost of not helping him find the mastermind. While they all knew the stories of how Nicholas and Tyrone had become O.G.'s in the first place, they didn't want any problems.

Nicholas was not a man who made idle threats, he said what he meant and did what he said. The leader of the Russian mafia, Victor, sat there with a smile on his face, thinking to himself, *"Why don't I just put a bullet in his head. What he did not wish to have was a war."* He too, was wondering who the shooter was, people around the table were wondering the same thing.

The Italian leader stated, "Well, I don't know who did it, however, I assure all of you my family had no hand in this. We will work with each of you to keep the peace. Aid in finding the one who ordered it, however, if any harm is done to our people or on our turf, we will not take it kindly."

Nicholas had talked earlier to Don Anthony and noted none of the Italian's ordered the hit. Nicholas wondered if someone at the table was responsible. Nobody wanted a war, blood was expensive. Not only did it cost men, war cost political clout, it turned the public against them.

The Chinese as well as the Japanese and Filipinos, for that matter, knew that war was awfully expensive. The Chinese were in a dispute with Drake Green, that had the city in a knot. The Japanese were just trying to find a place to move their products. They trafficked in exporting and importing young girls. The Filipino's really didn't have a dog in the hunt, they were caught in between the Chinese and the Japanese. They still had excellent connections for hashish, and they had a great deal of weapons.

After the meeting ended, they all left Polo's. Each made their way to their own cars and each had a lot on their mind and wanted to think about what was said.

***

Chapter 43

Thanksgiving was only a week away. Nina was in full panic mode as her parents and oldest Brother Eli and his wife Kate were due to arrive Tuesday afternoon. Nina hired a maid service to clean all the guest bedrooms and bathrooms. She instructed them to clean from top to bottom, not that it needed it, but just because her mother was coming.

Nicholas was going to physical therapy classes to get the full use of his left arm and hopefully work out stiffness he had in his back. Both Nick and Nina had been left with little nagging aches after the shooting. However, they were working through them as best they could.

Vivian called Nina about a wedding dress she saw. They were in the middle of planning a wedding for Christmas. They booked a Luxury nine night's cruise to Hawaii. It turned out that by taking a cruise instead of flying, they would be able to spend time on six islands while staying on the ship.

Nina, today, wanted to buy some new drapes and curtains for the master guest bedrooms. She was not pleased with what she had hanging in the rooms. She called Vivian, "Hi girl, what are you up to today? Feel like going shopping to look for some drapes and curtains?", asked Nina, in a soft voice.

"Hey to you, I was just thinking about going somewhere to get away from this house. Tyrone has been on a rampage yelling about the boy's going to San Jose before they talked to him. He knows they didn't do anything wrong, just that Tyrone still thinks of them as little boys, while they are men now. One day, one of them is going to slap him upside his head and tell him to sit his old ass down", said Vivian, with a little grin on her face.

"I hear that shit…If one of those little rug rats ever step to me, I'm goin put my foot in their ass, so far, it would take a month to get it out", said Tyrone, from the background.

"V, you know your big head man is not going to hurt those boys. He's just talking shit, they found out something he didn't, now his pride is hurt. I will be over to pick you up in an hour... Okay?", said Nina, with a smile on her face.

"I know you are right... I will be ready. We can also pick up Mia on the way. I told her the next time we were going shopping she could come. Might as well start today getting to know her," replied Vivian.

"Yes, I agree, I like her, she seems like a very nice woman, but that friend of hers, I can't take her for a moment."

"Yeah, I had to cuss her out one time, but I found out that she just has problems. She's cool, but she will not be going with us today."

They finished their conversation and hung up. Vivian went to get dressed and Nina called Mia.

"Hello... Who is this?"

"Hello Mia, this is Nina, how would you like to go shopping with Vivian and me today?"

"I would love to."

"Okay, be ready in an hour, we'll pick you up."

"By the way, what are we going shopping for?"

"Oh, I'm looking to freshen up the guest rooms for my parents who are coming for Thanksgiving."

"Okay, I'll be ready." Nina said her good-byes and hung up.

She made one more call and that was to James to get the limo, because she wanted him to drive them, that way they could talk and not worry about parking and driving.

***

The three women spent the afternoon browsing in and out of shops, ending up in a little drape shop in Hillsdale. They found two patterns they all agreed would work for the rooms. One for her parent's room and one for her brother and sister-in-law. Nina negotiated and haggled with the owner of the shop, until he agreed to have them installed by the end of business on Tuesday. It was going on five when they finished shopping and wanted to eat and Nina suggested they stop at Benihana's, which was her treat.

It was after eight when they dropped Mia at her house. JR had seen the note that Mia left, and he was sitting in the family room watching football when she walked in.

"How was your day?", he asked, as Mia planted a kiss on his cheek.

"I had a great time, how was your day?", she asked, as she took a bottle of water from the refrigerator.

"It was okay, nothing to talk about", said JR, not wanting to sound stressed.

Mia looked at him and replied, "I'm going up and take a hot bath, my feet are killing me from all the walking. Your mother and Vivian said hi.

Those two women can do some walking and shopping. I thought I was insane when I was looking for something special, but those two are the queens of shopping", she stated, as she made her way to the steps.

Vivian and Nina talked on the way to Vivian's about wedding plans and what they planned to fix for Thanksgiving dinner. Nina was having Mrs. Green cook a big dinner and having the whole family over.

By the time Nina got home, Nicholas was sitting in the bed with his head deep in some papers that Hazel had brought over, about the bank deal. No matter how hard she tried to keep him from working he would still find a way. She just looked at him and walked into the bathroom and turned on the hot water in the tub.

***

Nina's folks plane landed on time, Nina and Nick met them at the gate and walked to the baggage claim to get their luggage. Nina's father was impressed with the airport. He didn't like to fly but did it for his daughter. He liked the train because he liked to see the scenery and take his time.

His wife, Mary, on the other hand was an outgoing diva type. She loved being the big fish in a pond. She was loved by everyone in her neighborhood, her biggest fear was leaving her community. Mary's mother and her mother's family had lived in the same three blocks for over a hundred years. While her children had left the block, she did not plan to leave, ever.

Now, seeing California, was a new adventure for Mary. Not so for Johnny, Nina's father. He had been to California when he was in the army during the war. He tried to get Mary to move to California back then, but that never happened.

He was excited to see the old stomping grounds he used to get drunk on and stagger back to the base. He wanted to see where he had fun as a young man.

Nina's Brother Eli was used to traveling, he was impressed with Nicholas and the way he carried himself. Eli and Kate, his wife, were always on the go, due to the work Eli did as Sr. Vice President of mergers and acquisitions for Morgan Chase Bank International. Eli saw Nicholas as one in a million, who got out of the ghetto and made it.

Nicholas was still wearing a bandage on the left side of his face covering his left jaw. He was going to the dentist after Thanksgiving to check on the implants placed in his jaw bone. His face had healed fairly well. After two weeks at home from the hospital, he could talk a little better, but it still required a great deal of effort on his part.

They all got in the limo and instructed James to drive through the heart of town, showing them the lay of the land. They looked out the tinted windows at the city and hillside homes. When James turned onto the block that Nicholas and Nina lived on, they were impressed with the site of the six-bedroom house.

***

Nina took her mother and sister-in-law and showed them around, while the guys went to the family room. Nick fixed drinks for them and turned on the ball game. Nick showed them the little golf putting green he had installed, outside the den, on the lawn. He showed them the pool house with its own bar right next to the pool.

After they had seen the whole house, Mrs. Green, the housekeeper, told them that dinner would be ready in about an hour. Nina showed her mother the guest room for her. Her mother was impressed with the drapes and furnishings. That pleased the hell out of Nina. Her sister-in-law was a little envious, not in a bad way, because while she had a beautiful house, it was not as lavishly furnished or spacious as Nina's; Nina's taste was flawless!

* * *

The morning after they arrived, Mary got up at her usual time, five-thirty, and went to the kitchen. She found Nina was there cutting up some potatoes and frying bacon. She was busy cooking. Mary just stepped in and started to break eggs and helping, as they said good morning. Kate walked in wearing a silk robe and she too started to help.

By the time the men got down to the kitchen, the women had cooked breakfast and made coffee. The three women were sitting around the kitchen table drinking coffee and talking about family and friends.

Nicholas was the first one in the kitchen. He walked over to Nina, kissed her and said, "good morning," he then went out to the front porch to get his paper.

"Good morning to you", said Nina, which was echoed by her mother and Kate. Johnny walked in and asked for a cup of coffee. He said, "good morning everybody", and sat down in a big stuffed chair in the family room to drink his coffee.

Eli walked into the kitchen, "this house is large, I almost got lost trying to find the kitchen," said Eli, joking. He took a cup and poured some coffee while taking a piece of bacon and stood next to the counter. They all ate and talked about family and friends. Nicholas asked Johnny and Eli if they had any places they wanted to go or see.

"I want to go down to seventh street and see what it looks like," Johnny said, with a smile on his lips.

"I'm willing to follow along, I would like to go see the "Wall Street West", if we have the time, "said Eli, who had wanted to see what the west coast wall street looked like. Mainly because his bank was thinking about buying a bank in San Francisco, so he thought he would look at the place first hand. After all, they were only going to be here for two more days.

The women were going to go shopping and Nina and Vivian planned to take the company jet to LA for the day. Nina had invited Mia to go, so the three of them were going to show Mary and Kate Hollywood.

Mrs. Green, the housekeeper, walked in the back door and saw all the mess. "My Lord... Why yaw in my kitchen? You know you don't know how to cook right, get yourself up and out, so I can get started on that bird", said Mrs. Green, in a southern Louisiana, friendly voice, only old women had.

Mrs. Green had been working for Nina for two months and she had taken over the house. She told the pool man when he could clean the pool, and the gardener when he could blow the leaves. She ran the whole house, while Nina hired a maid company to do the heavy cleaning, Mrs. Green did most of the food shopping. Nina just shook her head and said, "We better get out before she really goes off in here."

***

E veryone was seated around the dining room table. The children were at the table in the kitchen, with the older kids sitting at the table and the younger ones at the little kids table. Nina asked her father to say grace and after he gave thanks for the meal, everyone started to eat. Mrs. Green had out done herself and the two people she got to help were great. The table looked beautiful and the food was cooked just as Nina had pictured. She had watched over the cooking and preparing of every dish.

Vivian and Tyrone were happy to see Nina happy, that her parents and brother were able to come. JR and Mia, Devon and Lydia and her son, Fred Jr., Bobby and his friend Jamaica, who had a daughter named Dianne, Roland and Maria; Charles and his girl Connie; Hazel and her friend Robert; Sandra and David, and their two kids, David Jr. and Cynthia from Sacramento; John and his girlfriend Tanesha, Frank and Olivia. For one moment they were all at peace enjoying each other, celebrating Thanksgiving, sharing stories with each other, dreaming of the future to come.

***

The next morning Nina took Mary to the day salon and lunch in the City. They spent the whole day doing mother daughter things. They looked at new coats and dresses, tried on new shoes and just enjoyed the company of each other. Mary loved to shop and was looking at all the shops she didn't have back home. She bought a couple of things, but mostly she loved being with her daughter. They were leaving for home the next morning, so they were going to just kick back at the house and talk for the rest of the night.

Vivian had invited Kate to go with her and Mia for the day. Kate also loved to shop but wanted to see some of the sites. She had a great interest in the Napa Valley wine country. She wanted to get some special wines and champagnes for her wine cellar. So, Vivian and Mia took her to Napa Valley on the train. They spent the whole day tasting wines. Kate ordered a couple cases of wine and three cases of

Nicholas II A Storm is Coming

champagne, to be shipped to her home. Vivian and Mia bought a couple of bottles of wine and they had lunch on the train.

***

The men had done everything they could think about. Johnny was so delighted to walk down memory lane. He told Nicholas, Tyrone, and Eli, about Seventh street during the war, and shared old war stories. Johnny was totally exhausted. When they got back to the house, he fell asleep in Nick's big chair in the family room. Eli and Nicholas went in Nick's den and talked for a couple of hours before Eli went to bed.

***

Nick went up to his bedroom to find Nina sitting at her vanity. She was combing and brushing her hair. He walked over and kissed her and said, "I love you", then walked in the bathroom, got a bottle of pills out the medicine cabinet and he took a pain pill. Nick came out of the bathroom and got in bed. Nina finished combing her hair and climbed in bed, sliding under Nicholas arm, and cuddled close to him. "Good night... and thank you for loving me, I love you so much", she said, and turned off the light. Nick wrapped his arm around her and closed his eyes. *"Thank you, God, for you have given me so much,"* he prayed, as he did every night.

***

The week after Thanksgiving Nicholas got word that Flip was located. Seems he was holed up in an apartment on the south side of Hayward. Turns out the apartment was the same address as the nurse. Nicholas and Tyrone started to put two and two together. They went to the address and watched the place for a couple of hours.

They didn't see anyone come out or go in the apartment while they were there. So, Nicholas decided to try another idea, he was going to see if he could get someone to knock on the door and see who was there. Luck had it that a young boy was sitting on the bench outside the place listening to music on a boombox.

Nicholas signaled for the boy to come to his car. When the young boy came over, Nicholas asked him if he wanted to make five dollars.

"Hell yeah, what I gotta do," replied the boy.

"Go up there and knock on apartment number 5 and ask for John", said Nicholas.

The boy took off running toward the stairs. He went to the door and knocked, he knocked a second time, and someone opened the door a little and asked, "Who is it and what do you want"?

"I'm looking for John," said the boy.

"There is nobody by that name here", said the voice behind the door and shut it.

The boy ran down the stairs to the car, and said, "they say there is no John up there".

Nicholas handed the boy a ten and told him he did good. Now that he knew someone was in the apartment, he and Tyrone would be able to get them out.

Checking their guns, Nicholas and Tyrone started up the steps and got to the apartment door. With a big foot on the lock, Tyrone kicked the door, causing it to fly in the apartment and he and Nicholas were right behind it with their guns held high. As soon as Tyrone entered the room, he saw Flip sitting at the table. "Don't even try it", said Tyrone to Flip, who wanted to reach for his gun on the table.

"Get up and move over there", said Tyrone, never taking his eyes off Flip.

Nicholas looked at Flip and said, " your friend is gone, and you are going to join her, if you don't start talking and tell me who sent you after me," said Nicholas, looking at Flip.

"I don't know what the fuck you are talking about. I'm not talking, you piece of shit, you killed my woman."

"Oh, so you're the fool that she was protecting. She sure knew how to pick them. You're not going to like the way I treat you, if you don't tell me what I want to know."

"Go to hell. I'm not telling you shit", replied Flip.

"Yeah, ok, we'll see if you are gangster or not... let's get him out of here before anyone comes along being nosy," said Nicholas to Tyrone.

"Yeah, let's get the fuck out of this stinking hell hole... How could you sit in here with that smell?", asked Tyrone, as he grabbed Flip, wrapping the duct tape around his hands and wrists and leading him out the apartment; they put Flip in the trunk of the car.

By the time they turned the corner the crackheads and junkies had started to remove everything in the apartment. They took everything in the place within ten minutes.

***

Once out at the ranch, Flip was tied to the same chair that Juanita had been in. He was trying to act all tough and hard, but in his heart, he knew he was scared. Nicholas and Tyrone stood over hm and looked down at him.

Well tough guy, ready to talk...or do we need to start with a little pain?" asked Tyrone, as he hit Flip in the mouth with the butt of his gun. Blood shot out along with two teeth, and Flip's head spun around to the right. The pain was unbearable as he screamed in agony.

"That was a wake-up tap...now are you ready to tell me who sent you?"

"I'm not telling you shit."

Before Flip could get the words out his mouth, Tyrone hit him again, this time Flip saw the hand coming and tried to brace for the pain, but it didn't help. The butt of the gun hitting his jaw caused two more teeth to fly across the room. Tyrone continued to ask Flip who sent him, and Flip continued to say, "fuck you."

"Okay...okay...let's move to the next step, he wants to make it hard... well so be it", said Nicholas, as he stood up and took a blow torch from the shelf and lit it.

Nickels moved around to where Flip could see him, with his one good eye. Flip saw Nickels lite the torch, then before he could react, his right cheek was burning. Flip turned his face to the left and his hair caught on fire. Nicholas moved the torch down to his chest and the hot flames burned his chest to the bone.

"Stop...stop... I'll talk...I'll talk", screamed Flip, through the pain. Nicholas looked at him and said, "No, you remember you said for me to fuck myself, you're not telling me shit, isn't that what you said", said Nicholas.

"No...No...No... I'll talk, just stop hurting me, said Flip.

With that, Flip opened his mouth and told Nicholas and Tyrone everything he knew. Tyrone just looked at him and thought about his woman who was more gangster than he was. She was true, he on the other hand was a fake-ass punk.

After they got the name of Flip's boss and everything Flip knew, Nicholas said, "I'm not going to shoot you or kill you. You are not worth a bullet. Tyrone, have John feed this nigga to the hogs."

"No...No...No... you said you weren't going to kill me", cried Flip.

Nicholas II A Storm is Coming

"I'm not going to kill you...the hogs are", said Nicholas, as he and Tyrone walked out the shed.

***

Nicholas and Tyrone left the ranch and headed back to Nicholas house. When they got there, they both went in the den and sat down and talked for an hour. Then Nicholas placed a call to Danny, the head of the Cartel.

"Hello Danny, it's Nick... you got a minute to talk?"

"Hello, my friend, yes, what is the problem."

"I need your permission to handle something".

"Well, let's meet tomorrow, at hanger three".

"Okay, I'll be there at nine".

"Alright, nine it is, said Danny, and hung up.

We need to call Thomas and get the plane ready. We are going to have to make a couple of stops, if everything goes right", said Nicholas.

"I'll pick you up at seven. Do you want to have Roland or Charles go with us?", asked Tyrone?

"No... just you and me. Look I have to make a couple of calls to make sure that other matter gets handled," said Nicholas, always thinking four steps ahead.

"Oh, on that, I have gotten all the information to the right people and everyone is ready. Just give them the word", said Tyrone, while looking at Nick with a smile.

"Yeah, my man, you are going to be a married man in a couple of days. Have you gotten everything for the trip?

"I got everything I need. That woman of mine has been shopping like she's got money in her veins; you know Nina has been right there, the two of them and JR's woman Mia have been buying out the stores."

197

"Yeah, that's what women do. They must have a different outfit for everything and like to have options.

The first time Nina and me went on a luxury cruise, she was mad because she didn't have the dress she wanted to wear for dining with the captain. After that, she makes sure she has two of everything she thinks she would wear. So, don't worry about them, let them do them and we can do us."

They both sat there and drank a cold beer and talked for a while. Tyrone got up and said, "hey Nick, I have to go check on the old girl and I will see you in the morning. We are getting to the end of this mess", said Tyrone, as he left Nick's, headed home.

The next morning, they arrived at the hanger and Danny and Jimmy were sitting there in their plane. Nicholas and Tyrone got out of Nick's plane and walked to Danny's plane and got in. Danny and Jimmy shook hands with Tyrone and Nicholas as they sat down.

"Well my friend, what is the problem that we had to come here in person", said Danny, happy to see Nicholas up and well.

"First, thank you for coming. I found out who the mastermind was behind the attempt on my life."

"Who was it? Have you taken care of them yet?", asked Jimmy, butting in.

"Yes, who did it?", replied Danny.

"It was Carlos... out of El Paso and a woman named Carmella, a Colombian, who he is fucking. Carlos planned to buy from her after I was out the picture, then they could move into Cali", said Nicholas, looking Danny in the eye with a sincere look.

"You got to be shitting me... Carlos is a snake and all, but to go behind my back and disrespect me like that...I will kill him myself", said Danny, in a fit of rage.

"I have it on good authority, that it was Carlos, even the man I know who works for him confirmed it. Seems Carlos has been fucking the Colombian woman named Carmella. She is from the east coast and bad news from what I hear. Her son has almost taken over Houston and she is moving to take over the west coast.

"So, we have a war coming," said Jimmy.

"Not if you let me handle Carlos. I have a plan in place that will end the whole mess, if you allow me to handle it."

After talking for about an *hour,* and going back and forth, about how best to get at Carlos and Carmella; Nicholas explained his plan to Danny and Jimmy. Danny said okay and told Nicholas he was in charge and to let him know when it was done. With that, they all said their good-byes and left.

***

Vivian was a nervous wreck with the wedding only days away. Nina , Mia, and she were shopping and hunting down outfits for the cruise as well as the wedding. Mia had made sure that everyone that was going to the wedding had a room at the Hilton and that they had their ticket to Hawaii. She and JR and Devon and Lydia were flying in the day before, so they could go see some sites. The rest of the crew were getting in the morning of the wedding. Nina had made sure that Vivian's dress was finished and shipped to the hotel by FedEx and she made sure the bridesmaid dresses were shipped. The beauticians and makeup personnel were flying in the day before the wedding, in order to get everyone ready the morning of. Vivian was glad she had bought Tyrone's ring and gifts for the bridesmaids on one of their shopping sprees. Everything was coming together just as she planned it.

Nina only had a couple more things to check on with the wedding coordinator; and one was to check with the bakery making the wedding cake, to be sure delivery was on schedule, and to call the flower shop and make sure the flowers were ready; she definitely wanted the flowers that were popular in Hawaii and had that aroma you can only smell on the island. Then she thought about the fact that Mrs. Green would be getting back from her trip to see her great grandchildren, the same day they leave on the cruise.

So, she needed to leave her some money. Mrs. Green was now like the mother of the house and she took care of everything for them; what a blessing!

***

The Saturday before the cruise Nicholas and Tyrone were at the Warrior's game watching them get beat again. They could not believe that the warriors were going to miss the playoffs again.

"How is everything going?"

"Everybody is ready, and things are taken care of. Everybody has an alibi, everybody's been paid", stated Tyrone.

"Good, now let's get home and get a good night's sleep because we have to fly in the morning".

"Okay... my man... I'll see you tomorrow... Oh yeah, come to the car for a minute, I wanna give you something," replied Tyrone, with a slight grin.

"What do you have in the car, what you wanna give me?", asked Nick, a little surprised.

Walking to the car, Tyrone opened his trunk and handed Nick a box, telling him, "don't open this until you get home." Nick took the box, curious as to its contents, but put it in his trunk and drove home. When he got in the house, he opened it to find a new bulletproof vest, and smiled to himself. He went upstairs, took a hot shower, and climbed in bed with Nina to get a good night's sleep.

***

Breaking News: Jimmy Fat Lou, leader of the Chinese gang, was found shot in the head outside his home early this morning. In the south bay, the body of Willie, little boy Edwards, the leader of the Filipino gangs, was found dead on the steps of his apartment, shot three times in the back and head.

At Fisherman's Wharf here in the city, two of the Godfathers of the Italian mafia were found dead, hanging from the mast of a fisherman's boat. No names have been released. Richmond police reported the murder of Victor Vasolev, head of the Russian mafia. He was found in his car with his throat cut, early this morning.

All the police departments are withholding information and comments, the FBI has been called in to investigate. We can only speculate, but it appears to be underworld related. These five murders bring the total murders in the bay area this year to over 344.

In other news, the Warriors lose to the Lakers for the fifth time this season. The A's signed Mel Russell to a new deal for 1.2 million over two years. We will be right back after a word from our sponsors; they cut to a commercial. Nickels turned the radio off and started to think about his next move.

Nicholas and Tyrone listened to the news reporter as they headed to the Oakland Executive Airport to fly to Houston. They boarded the gulf stream plane, got comfortable in the big chairs and waited for Dotty, the attendant, to bring them a drink. The gulf stream received clearance to take off.

Thomas, Chief pilot for Simmons company, announced they would be climbing to a cruising altitude of thirty-eight thousand. He also informed them they would be in Houston, in approximately an hour and forty minutes.

Nicholas and Tyrone sat back and enjoyed their drinks. They discussed some of the details about the upcoming events. Nicholas was in his own mind going over strategies and scenarios, while Tyrone was thinking how proud he was the crew had handled themselves so well.

***

Two hours later they were touching down in Houston, where a car was waiting for them. They got in a rented limo and headed to the Body Shop Club. They walked into the club and went straight to the main office. Flip's lieutenant, Ricky, was standing behind the desk with his dick in his hand, with a dancer laying on the desk. Tyrone walked in and pulled his 45 and shot him and her two times in the head, turned and walked out like nothing happened, got back in the limo, and drove off.

The next stop was a Mexican restaurant on the south side where they both walked in and shot Roberto Hernandez, the son of Carmella Hernandez, Head of the Colombian Cartel in Miami. They shot five of Roberto's men along with three women sitting with them. They missed Carmella by thirty minutes. She had taken a flight to Miami that morning. Nicholas didn't like the fact that she got away.

They drove back to the airport and boarded the plane and were in the air in less than two hours. The plane's next touchdown was in El Paso, Texas. They got in a limo, sent by their host, the head of the Cartel in El Paso. He had been told that Nicholas and Tyrone were going to meet someone from Mexico. He was given the reason; it was not a good time to meet in California because of the DEA.

Danny had instructed Carlos to host their meeting in his city. Carlos had no choice in the matter but thought it would be the perfect opportunity to kill both Nicholas and Tyrone. He could blame it on any number of gangs in the area. He set it up to have them brought to his hacienda.

He thought with them gone he could then make his move, then go after Danny and Jimmy. Then he and Carmella could take over the whole west coast and run the whole thing from coast to coast.

When Nicholas and Tyrone got to Carlos's hacienda, they were shown to the patio and pool area. Carlos was sitting out by the pool with two young women who were nude, swimming and playing in the pool.

"Hello, my friend", said Carlos, as he got up to shake their hands.

"Hello to you Carlos, long time no see", said Nicholas, shaking his hand.

"Hi, Carlos, nice to see you", said Tyrone, in a voice that sounded like he was happy to see him.

Carlos thought to himself, "*I got them now, I just have to play it cool for a few hours, and then kill them and blame it on someone.*"

Nicholas II A Storm is Coming

"How was your trip, and by the way, what time is the meeting to start. I want to tell the chefs, so they are ready, said Carlos, trying to hide what he had planned.

"The meeting will start in about a minute, said Nicholas, as he turned toward one of Carlos's men and nodded at him in a way that signaled to move towards Carlos.

"Take a seat Carlos, we need to talk about something", said Nicholas. Carlos's man turned to him and took the gun out of Carlos's pants, as he pulled his own gun and pointed it at Carlos. Totally surprised by the action, Carlos was in total shock, when he started to open his mouth to talk; Tyrone pulled his gun, slapped Carlos across the lips, and shot the guard that was standing next to Carlos, while the two ho's by the pool heard the shot and ducked.

"What the hell's going on", said Carlos, after grabbing his face.

"I know you were the one who orchestrated the shooting of me and Nina", said Nicholas.

"I had nothing to do with that, what the fuck is going on, I let you in my house and you accuse me of masterminding something."

"I don't have a lot of time, so I will make this quick, I have never liked or disliked you until you started to treat me like shit. Now you can come clean like a man or go out like the punk-ass snake you are. Your own men don't like you, and Danny has given me permission to end it.

"You are fucking crazy, I'm the son of the founder of the Cartel, you can't take me out. I run this shit up in here. He turned and started to yell for some other men to help. Four men ran into the patio and stood there looking at him like they were mad.

"Now let me show you what real power looks like Carlos. It will be the last thing you see or hear", said Nicholas, as he turned around and headed toward the car.

"Shoot him and then burn his body", said Nicholas.

The four men opened fire and shot Carlos, who's body flew in the air and hit the ground. Carlos, however, didn't hear the shot that killed

203

him because the first shot hit him in the head, and he was dead before his body knew it. But they kept on firing until all four had emptied their clips into him.

"Nicholas and Tyrone had left the gate of the hacienda before they finished shooting Carlos, and the two ho's that were unlucky to be in the pool.

Back on the plane, Nicholas and Tyrone had a glass of Hennessy, as the plane headed to Cali. Landing at the Livermore airport and getting in the limo, they headed to Oakland International Airport to catch a plane, with Nina and Vivian, to Vancouver to begin their cruise.

***

Chapter 46

Nina and Vivian sat in first class and talked about the wedding, and if they had gotten everything for the trip. Nicholas and Tyrone just sat back and relaxed knowing that their enemies had been eliminated. Well, at least all but Carmella, Nicholas knew he was going to have to deal with her very soon. He could not let her go on living for very long, or it would bite him in the ass. Nicholas also thought about Drake Green and his part in this. After the trip he was going to deal with both of them.

When the plane landed, they got in a limo which took them to the ship's port. Once the four of them saw the ship for the first time, they were surprised at the size and beauty of the ship and the dock area.

It was bigger than Nick thought it would be. They had both booked one-bedroom deluxe suites on the tenth deck with patio's. Their personal steward met them at the ticket counter check point, taking them out of the line and aided them through the VIP section. He informed them that their luggage was going aboard and would be placed in their Suite.

Nina and Vivian looked around in the little shops on the dock before getting on the ship. The two of them walked around the shops on the ship for a few moments, just looking and mapping out the ship.

Wanting to see the Suite, both couples made their way to the tenth deck and found their suites. Nicholas and Nina were in 1066 and Tyrone and Vivian were in 1068.

The Suite was incredibly beautiful, and the decor and the ocean view were fantastic. They had requested one-bedroom suites with patios on the port side of the ship. Living rooms and bathrooms were very exquisite, and the gifts Nick picked for Nina were spread out all over the living room. Flowers, chocolate, and a big fruit basket. Nicholas had a banner printed which read, "Happy Retirement" and one in the bedroom that said, "I Love You Nina", which was hanging, when Nina saw it, she gave him a big wet kiss on the lips.

Tyrone and Vivian's room was laid out in the same manner and had all the amenities that Nick and Nina had. Nick and Nina had gotten a banner printed for them, that read "Congratulations" as well as the one with "Happy Retirement."

***

For the next three days they would be on the ocean. The first port of call was Hawaii and there they would be leaving the ship and going to the Grand Hilton Hotel for a two-night stay and the wedding. Friends and family were already staying there waiting for them to arrive. The four of them had dinner that night on the ship. After dinner they went to a show and listened to some jazz in the lounge. Nina and Nick took a walk around the deck just looking at the sites and the ocean. When they got back to their Suite they sat out on the patio and talked.

The next morning, they all met in the dining room and talked about what they were going to do. The women said they had booked time at the spa and that they were going to attend an art exhibit, browse around, and then lay by the pool. Nick and Tyrone decided they would go to the gym, and then to the bar and watch sports, and drink a beer or two.

The second night out at sea, they had dinner with the Captain and his guests. Nina wore a gown made by Christian Dior and Vivian wore one made for her by Ferragamo. To say they were the best dressed women on the ship is an understatement. Nick and Tyrone had on black designer tuxedos by Ralph Lauren; Nick was also sporting his Patek Phillipe Grand Complications watch and Tyrone had on his Girard Perregaux, 18 k gold watch, with an alligator strap, an early wedding gift from Nick and Nina; the occasion seemed to call for a little flash, thought Nick.

The women were happy and having fun. After dinner they went to the Casino where Nick and Tyrone taught the girls how to shoot craps and play roulette. Vivian won five hundred on the crap table and Nina picked up a cool thousand on the roulette wheel.

***

Nicholas II A Storm is Coming

The third day out they saw some whales over the side of the ship and watched them swim along. They saw a fishing boat pulling in a net full of tuna. But mostly they watched the day go by and enjoyed the time together. The ship made port about five in the morning. When Nina and Nick woke up, they had docked, and the crew was busy re-supplying the ship. They showered and got dressed, preparing to go ashore for the next two days, while the ship was going to be docked. Nina and Nick ate and drank the coffee and honey buns brought to them by their steward. He had left them on the table in the little dining area. The plan was for Tyrone and Vivian to get married on shore and then honeymoon on the cruise ship. They were going to four other islands, before returning to Vancouver.

***

The three days went by so fast that they didn't realize it. Tyrone and Vivian spent most of their time in their room acting like children. They had been on the ship for three days, now they were going to leave and go to the Grand Hilton for their wedding.

When they got to the Hotel, the Wedding Coordinator met with Vivian and Nina for about an hour, going over all the plans for the wedding. Nick and the fellows took off for parts unknown. It was Nicholas and JR's job to keep Tyrone busy for the day. So, JR and Devon had found a strip club for them to start at and then they were going to a hotel by Pearl Harbor for the night. Bobby hired five strippers to come to the hotel and party. All in all, they were going to send Tyrone off in style.

Nina and Vivian were busy getting the last-minute things for the wedding done. Mia and Lydia were busy getting the party ready for Vivian. They hired a couple of male strippers and ordered some food and drinks for Vivian's party. Mia was footing the bill because of the love she had for Vivian and Nina.

Both groups had a blast, the men partied and lied about women, and drank too much. The women had a great time partying with the two-male strippers, giving Vivian all kinds of sexy gifts for her wedding night, eating food and drinking, and telling lies about men.

A B Hudson

By the time, the wedding was to start, they were all dressed in their best, well groomed, and ready for the show. Vivian had asked Roland to walk her down the aisle. Her father had died some years ago. Roland did a great job and Maria was so proud of him she started crying. She was also thinking about when her and Roland were going to jump the broom. The wedding went exactly like Nina and Vivian had planned. The reception went off without a hitch. They partied and danced most of the evening in the ballroom they had rented. They even got Tyrone to get up and dance, once. Everyone was happy and full of joy.

Tyrone and Vivian were so happy and in love and showed it. Who would have thought these two would get married? Tyrone was a true O.G. and one of the meanest men to walk the streets. Nicholas was so proud of his partner; he could hardly contain his pride.

The next morning Vivian, Tyrone, Nicholas and Nina said goodbye, to those who made the parting breakfast, or to those sober enough to get up, before they returned to the ship to continue the cruise. Nicholas Junior and Mia had been on the island for 3 days, they were going to see a couple more islands and spend another week before returning to the mainland. Roland and Maria decided that they were going to go to the island of Maui, just so she could see it. They were going to do a little tourist sightseeing. Devon and Lydia were heading back to the mainland, Lydia had to go deal with her baby's daddy; a dude called big Fred, who was raising hell about not seeing his son, which pissed Devon off to no extent. The rest of the family had made their own plans, everyone was going in different directions at different times.

***

Nina and Vivian talked for a moment back on the ship. Vivian told her she would see her at dinner and Vivian said, "You may not be able to walk to dinner," with a smile on her face.

"Girl hush your mouth, you know I'm not like that", said Vivian, with a grin on her face; but as the newly wed Mrs. Vivian Lawson, I'm gonna treat my man right!

208

Nicholas II A Storm is Coming

"Well, you have fun, and I will see you when I see you," said Nina, and started toward her room. Nick was sitting on the sofa reading one of the books he had brought, catching up on his reading. He got up when she came in and walked over and gave her a kiss on the lips.

"I'm glad that's over, and they are happy. Now we can get down to the matter of getting this bank under control and retire ourselves and get out the game. When we get back, I'm going to the office and start getting a handle on the business."

"Nick, we are on vacation, just stop with the work and relax and have some fun. I would like to go down to the casino and try to learn how to play blackjack and then go dancing. Is that too much to ask?", said Nina.

"No, baby, I just get rapped up in my work, I forget that you don't think the way I do. Let's put on some clothes and go. I'll show you how to play blackjack and then I'm going to get you high and take advantage of you later", said Nick, with a sexy look on his face.

"Oh, you are, well let's see who takes advantage of who", said Nina, with a sexy look of her own.

They both kissed and left the room holding hands as they made their way to the casino and club.

***

The day they returned to Vancouver and left for home, the weather had turned, and it was getting cold. They were happy to get back on dry land, and happy they would be back in Oaktown, in a couple of hours. During the last two days of the trip Nicholas had relaxed and for a moment had forgot about dealing with Carmella, and Drake and Oscar. And spent the rest of the trip romancing and enjoying Nina.

***

Mrs. Green was in her apartment when they got to the house. She came out and met them at the door of the living room. She gave each of them a big hug and told them how she missed them. Charles took their bags up to the master suite; he came down and told Nicholas that he needed to talk to him. Nina and Mrs. Green went into the kitchen, she and Nina were able to sit and talk about the trip and all the tea on the wedding, while Charles and Nick went to his den.

In the den, Nick went to his bar and got a drink and asked Charles if he wanted one. He said, "yes, I would," so Nick poured him one, and they sat down in the chairs in front of his desk.

"What is it that you need to talk about?", asked Nick.

"I just wanted to give you an update", answered Charles.

"Okay, what's happening? Did you do like I asked in my wire?", asked Nick.

"Yeah, we were able to find out she went to New York, and then back here to see that dude Drake Green over in Hunter's Point."

"Wait a minute, you telling me she is working with Drake?", asked Nick, surprised somewhat by Charles statement.

"Yeah boss, him and her have been running all over the city, word has it."

"And what else have you been able to get hold of?"

"While the police have been looking for the killers of the leaders of the families and gangs, they have come up with nothing, I hear from our inside people."

"I'm not surprised at that; I knew they would not look too hard. But I want to know who is stepping up to fill the shoes of the one's gone."

"We are on it, but no word yet on anybody making any moves."

"Okay, I'm going into the office tomorrow, I want to meet with the crew tomorrow at eight, so let everyone know."

With that said, Nick told Charles they would talk in the morning, he was going to get some rest. The fact was Nick wanted to think and figure out how he was going to deal with Carmella and Drake.

Nicholas II A Storm is Coming

He didn't realize Carmella was fucking Drake, as well as Carlos, but it made good business. If she got Drake to help her, she would have a foot in the door. If not, she was no better or worse off.

Nicholas got up early and got dressed to go into the office for the first time since the shooting. He wanted to see how things were going and to get his head in the game. James drove him to the office, where he got out in the garage and took the elevator to the twenty-fifth floor. He walked in the double doors of his outer office. The rich mahogany wood doors and tan oak panel with chrome and tan furniture, gave the office a great décor. His secretary was not at her desk as he approached, so he continued into his office, shutting the door as he entered. His secretary, Miss Barbara Jackson, had been getting a cup of coffee and she was not aware of Mr. Simmons coming in. When she got back to her desk and saw that the light on his phone was on, she called security to investigate. The guard walked in and saw it was Mr. Simmons, and said, "Excuse me Sir, we got a call. I will cut off the alarm, you have a good day."

"It's alright young man, Miss Jackson was not at her desk when I came in."

Miss Jackson came rushing in when she heard his voice and apologized for calling security.

"I'm so happy to see you. You look great and I'm sorry I was away from my desk when you got here", said Miss Jackson.

"That's okay, I should have given you a heads up, that I was coming in today."

After the guard left and they were alone, she asked him if he wanted some coffee or water. Nicholas told her he was fine and that he would be going over some papers and making some calls for about an hour or so.

"It was afternoon when Nicholas finished reading the documents and making the calls he wanted made.

***

Nicholas had a half ham sandwich with a garden salad, for lunch, at the café around the corner from the office. Returning to the office, he called Miss Jackson and asked her to have JR come to his office.

"Mr. Simmons, your father would like for you to come to his office," said Barbara, into the phone.

"Okay, I didn't know he was in the office. Tell him I'm on the way," said, JR. He then turned to the salesman in his office, "You'll have to excuse me, I will meet with you tomorrow, about the cell phones."

"Great, Mr. Simmons, I will see you tomorrow, remember; I have a great deal for you", said the salesman.

JR got up and walked the salesman to the front desk, continued to the other end of the office, and took the stairs up two floors to his father's, and was standing in front of Miss Jackson's desk. She looked at him and picked up her phone, "Your son is here Mr. Simmons", said Barbara, with a smooth voice.

"Send him in", said Nicholas.

"Hey Pop's, what brings you to the office?", asked JR, with a little smile.

"I own the joint, that's why", said Nicholas, half joking.

"You look good, and I'm glad you are back in the saddle, ready to work."

"That's what I want to talk to you about. I think it's time I let you have the shield and I step aside. I'm retiring", said Nicholas, as he opened the left drawer in his desk, took out the shield his father had given to him many years ago. Now he was about to pass it to his son.

JR looked at the shield, and then up at his father. He wanted to say something but could not come up with any words. He just stood there like a deer caught in headlights. After he got over the shock, he said, "thank you, are you sure you want to retire?"

"Yes, I'm damn sure. Now take this and run the company, just as soon as I leave, which will be very soon."

Nicholas pulled JR in and gave him a hug. JR walked out the office with the family shield, that matched the ring he and his brothers wore on their right index finger, and with the knowledge that he was going to sit in the big chair, soon.

***

Nicholas had found that Carmella and Drake were seeing each other as both lover's and partners. Carmella wanted to kill Nicholas now for many reasons, but mainly because he had killed her son. She was going to use Drake to draw Nicholas out and then kill him.

Nicholas was busy making plans to remove the both of them. He had them watched, paid to have them followed, to learn their habits. He found they went to a couple of places that he thought he could use.

One place they would go every Thursday was to a little playhouse in the North Point area. Seems Carmella likes plays and she would go to them often. The second was a spa near Union Square, where she got her nails and hair done; Drake would go with her to get his toenails cut.

Nicholas decided the better spot was the day spa, and set up to take them out Saturday, when they came to the spa.

As Drake drove up to the alley where the day spa was located, a parking spot opened on the street, in front of his new 1986 Cadillac. North of them, five blocks away, a man was sitting on a building's roof, looking at the square with a high-powered, military scoped sniper rifle, with a heavy silencer. Also, south of them, five blocks away a second man was sitting on the roof of a building with the same type of rifle, looking at them pull into the parking spot. Both men carried walkie talkies, allowing them to communicate.

"I have the target, I'll take my shot when he steps out of the car", said Nick, while looking through the scope at Drake in the driver's seat of the 1986 blue Cadillac.

"Roger that, yeah, I have my target in sight, as soon as she opens the door, I'm gonna open her head", said Tyrone, from the roof top.

Just as he finished his transmission to Nick, Carmella opened the door of the 86 blue Caddy. She managed to get one foot on the ground. The heavy .762 caliber slug hit her on the right side of her temple, knocking her back into the car, as the slug and her brains and bone matter continued through the windshield and entered the engine block.

Almost simultaneously, before Drake could turn his head, a slug hit him at the base of his neck and knocked him almost completely out of the passenger's side of the blue caddy, taking his brains and bone with it to the ground. Neither one of them, Drake or Carmella, heard the shot. For that matter, no one in Union Square heard a sound. They were both dead before their bodies hit the ground.

Nicholas and Tyrone picked up their casing, broke down the rifles, and walked down the building fire escapes. They got in their respective cars and drove off, leaving mass confusion and terrified people five blocks away.

***

Oscar had been able to get out the hospital, and for the moment, hide out in Seaside with his girl Jackie and Poncho. Over the past two weeks Poncho had been looking for a new connect for them. He found a guy in Seaside who said he knew a big dealer he could get weight from. Oscar set up a meeting to meet the dude and see if he was real. They met in a little place out by the race track in Fremont.

Frank had Jewel and Big John with him. Oscar, Poncho, and Jackie drove up and parked. Jackie stayed in the car, as Oscar and Poncho got out and walked over to the place where Frank and Big John were standing. They talked for about three minutes.

Nicholas II A Storm is Coming

Frank told Oscar, that it would cost him seventeen a key, and that he didn't do less than four keys.

Oscar said, that's cool, and that he would take four keys. They agreed to get them the next day. Frank told him to have the money and that he would tell him where to go.

"Bring the money here at two o'clock. If you are not here at two, the product will be gone, understand?", said Frank.

"You're going to bring the product here at two tomorrow"? asked Poncho.

"No, you are going to bring the money here at two. The product will be in a car parked in the parking lot. After I get the money, I will tell you the location and give you the keys."

Okay, I get it, you don't trust me," said Oscar.

"I don't trust my mother when it comes to my freedom and money. So, you can do it my way, or hit the highway. I don't care one way or the other", said Frank.

The next day Frank and Big John were waiting at two for Oscar and Poncho to get there at two. The deal went as it was supposed to. That was the start of the Oscar, Frank, connection.

For the next two months Oscar took over San Jose and most of south San Francisco with product bought from Frank. By July, He was up to buying six keys twice a week.

Oscar was about to make a mistake, which was going to cost him. He decided he wanted to move in on the spot, that Drake's murder left open. He wanted to move into San Francisco. That caught the attention of Nicholas and Tyrone who wanted to know who this new player was.

They started to look into the dealers who were moving any weight and where they were getting their product.

Oscar had learned from his mistake before and Insulated himself from the street level. He now had over twenty people running houses, from

South San Francisco, up and down the Peninsula. His game was strong, crack had taken over. One could not get enough on the streets. Police were giving up, they only showed up to count the bodies.

***

The day was here that Nichols was stepping down, the whole crew had been planning this day for a year. Now October 1986 and the legend O.G. Nicholas Simmons was leaving the drug game.

Tyrone and JR had rented a house in the Oakland Hills to hold a private party. Only the crew and closest friends were invited. Security was tight, Tyrone didn't want any kind of surprises or problems. Nicholas was against the party, but he allowed it anyway, cause Nina said, let them honor you.

Like everything in the streets, it's hard to keep a secret. If one person knew, then it was not a sure bet. Nick still had enemies, tonight, one of them, saw a possible opportunity.

Making their way up the hill from the back side of the house, eight men with automatic assault rifles, wearing black, approached the house. Their plan was about to start when about 50 yards from the house, one of the eight stepped on a bouncing betty land mine, blowing him sky high. That forced them to start their assault. Tyrone had anticipated someone coming for them, so he had the back of the house mined. Tyrone, Nicholas, and his sons went into survival mode, drawing from the training and knowledge that Old John had taught them.

Taking defensive positions, they started working and moving like a well-oiled machine. Tyrone dropped behind a column on the porch and took two of the approaching assailants out. Nicholas, Jr. squatted down behind a patio chair, and took out one assailant as he passed, another coming up the steps. Nicholas, meanwhile, inside the patio door took aim and dropped two men as they came over the crest of the hill.

When the smoke cleared, seven assailants were dead, and three of Nicholas' people in the house. Tyrone grabbed one of the assailants

Nicholas II A Storm is Coming

and knocked him out, dragging him to the car. Tyrone was yelling Nick's name, "where are you Nick, trying to see through the smoke. He started looking at bodies laid out on the ground. Then hearing the police sirens, he knew he had to get lost. Everyone moving was trying to get away. As Tyrone, Nicholas, and JR, headed to the car, Nicholas came around the corner of the house and jumped in the back seat.

Tyrone turned the corner, going the opposite direction of the sirens, before the first car arrived.

Two blocks away from the house, Tyrone was driving and asked, "is everyone okay, is any one hit"?

"No, I'm not hit, JR, are you okay"? replied Nicholas, with a concerned voice.

"I'm fine, but what the hell was that…. who the fuck was that coming up the hill"?

said JR, with a puzzled look in his eyes.

"I had a hunch and a gut feeling that something was gonna go wrong", said Tyrone.

"What I don't understand is who were they".

"Well, we'll find out exactly who it was, because we have one in the trunk. Wait until we get him out at the ranch, he'll talk", said Tyrone, with a raging degree of anger in his voice.

"You telling me you got one in the trunk, said Nicholas, in a surprising manner. Did all of our people make it out."

"Pops, I don't know, I think I saw Roland and Frank make it out the front. All hell was breaking out, so I was ducking…I know I saw Willie G out of the village, I know he's gone…but I didn't see anyone else", said JR, from the front seat.

"What about your brothers, Devon and Bobby, did you see them?"

"I saw Devon in the living room, I don't know where Bobby was", said Tyrone.

A B Hudson

As Tyrone turned onto the freeway, he saw several police cars with sirens blasting headed up the hill. Two miles ahead of him, Devon, Bobby and Roland were headed towards Tracy. Nicholas sat back in the seat, put his hands over his eyes and thought to himself, *"I knew I should not have allowed them to throw a party. If any one of those boys are gone, Nina is gonna have my ass. Not to mention, I'll have to deal with Gloria."* He snaps out of his thoughts, takes his phone, and calls the house. The phone rings twice before Nina picks it up, "hello".

"Hello", babe, have you heard the news"?

"No, I wasn't looking at TV, I've been reading.

"Have any of the boys called? Before you hear it, I wanna let you know someone shot up the party; no, I don't know if everybody is okay, JR and Tyrone are with me and were headed out to the ranch. I'll give you a call when I know more".

"What you mean, shot up the party, what about Devon and Bobby, where are they"?

"I don't know right now, so let me get off the phone and let me find out."

"Okay, get back to me, do I need to get a hold of Vivian and Mia, get them over here, or are they cool.

"Right now, stay where you're at, I'll talk to you in a minute", Nicholas said, as he ended the call.

Tyrone pulled off the main road headed to the ranch. He pulled up to a parking spot next to Devon's car. "Hey, that's Devon's car," said Tyrone, in an excited voice.

As they were getting out the car, Devon, Bobby, and Roland walked out on the porch with John. Nicholas, seeing his two sons standing on the porch, let out a sigh of relief. After explaining that they had made it out the house, and had seen Frank and John headed towards Berkeley, Nicholas was greatly relieved, but still concerned about who may not have made it out.

218

Nicholas II A Storm is Coming

Taking the assailant out of the trunk and into the shed, they tied him to a chair.

Nicholas, still at the little house, told Devon to get on his phone and to find out if everyone made it out okay. Then he left and joined Tyrone in the shed. Neither one of them was in a good mood, they had both entered monster mode and were determined to have their way. Nicholas' only dream was he wanted out, yet some fool could not let the monster rest, so now it was time for the answers, and someone was going to pay. And the two legendary O.G.'s were going to get to the bottom of it.

"Wake the fuck up", said Nicholas, as he slapped the assailant.

"Yeah, wake the fuck up, it's time to talk", said Tyrone.

The assailant woke up from the pain of his jaw being hit by the butt of a 45.

"I don't know what the fuck you are hitting me for, I'm not going to talk, so you may as will kill me now, and be done."

"Yeah, that is what they always say, then we see if they are real, said Tyrone."

I'll be happy to make you talk but believe me it will take a minute to kill you. Now I want to know who sent you."

"Fuck yourself, I'm not talking."

To be continued